MISADVENTURES

WITH MY
ROOMMATE

BY
ELIZABETH HAYLEY

MISADVENTURES WITH MY ROOMMATE

BY
ELIZABETH HAYLEY

WATERHOUSE PRESS

To everyone who never got a chance to bang a hot roommate. This one's for you.

CHAPTER ONE

Blake moved her eyes with the crowd that bustled past The Coffee Bean. She'd been working for about three hours—the first two of which she'd spent listening to some girl whose name she couldn't remember introduce products and procedures at warp speed. Now she was thankful for the wall of windows that faced the busy street. Her mind wandered with the people outside, making up stories about who they were, where they'd come from, and where they were going.

A woman in a hot-pink miniskirt hobbled past in chunky black boots that laced up her calves. She'd clearly spent the night being ridden hard by a cowboy who'd come to town with a fictional rodeo. He'd roped her from his horse, stole away with her to his RV, and promised to look her up the next time his caravan rode through town. But he wouldn't, and she'd be left alone, looking forlornly down random streets as the memories of the fierce fucking he'd given her swamped her mind at the most inopportune times. Blake shook her head. She almost felt bad for Pink Miniskirt. Hers would be a difficult life.

"Excuse me, Miss. Miss!"

Blake came back to herself with a start. Blinking rapidly, she focused on the woman in front of her—a lady with a severe black bun and a tweed suit.

"Sorry," Blake said. A wide smile overtook her face as she continued. "How may I help you today?"

Black Bun didn't return the smile. Instead, she looked harried and irritated.

Blake instantly grew wary of this woman who looked like the fate of everyone she encountered that day depended on whether or not she got a giant container of coffee—though it made Blake feel a bit like a superhero barista. With this one order, she would be saving this woman's coworkers from being murdered with office supplies.

"I need a..."

And that was where Blake's understanding of Black Bun's order ended and her confusion began. The woman rattled off a combination of unfamiliar words with such speed that Blake wondered if the terms even applied to coffee. Surely there was no way *all* these words could be foreign to her. Though the woman ended her request with "latte," a word Blake understood, it did nothing to clarify exactly what she was supposed to be making for this person.

"I'm sorry, what?"

Black Bun repeated her order, but the result was the same. Blake turned and stared at the giant menu posted on the wall behind the counter in hopes that she'd see something that resembled the woman's order. No luck. Blake turned around slowly and stared at the woman awkwardly, unsure if asking her to repeat it again was worth either of their time.

"Jesus Christ," Black Bun muttered. "I just want a grande quad nonfat one-pump no-whip mocha latte."

This time, Blake heard all the words, but they meant

nothing to her when strung all together like that. Blake put her palms on the counter and leaned on them. "That's not a thing. I refuse to believe it."

The woman gritted her teeth. "Do you have a manager?"

"Probably," Blake replied. She figured the guy who had hired her was a manager, but she didn't remember what he'd said his exact title was.

Black Bun's face began turning an unnatural shade of red. "Can you get them?"

"Sure," Blake said brightly. That was something she could actually help with. Kind of. She turned to address the three other employees she'd been working with that day. "Do we have a manager, and more importantly, is the manager here?"

They all stared at her as if she'd asked them to solve Hammurabi's Code.

"Yeah, Stu's in back," a voice behind her said.

Blake whirled around to see the cute blond guy who'd been wiping off tables. He twisted a rag in his hands, making his forearms bunch. His was the only name she cared to remember because he was so hot. *Gavin*.

"I can get him for you," Gavin continued.

"Great. Thanks," Blake replied as Gavin started to walk off. "He's going to get him," Blake said to Black Bun.

The woman eyed her warily. "Is something wrong with you?"

Blake had heard this question a lot through the years, and it had stopped offending her a long time ago, especially since, yes, according to multiple medical professionals, there was something most definitely wrong with her. But Blake had also learned that people rarely wanted her to answer honestly, and even though Blake didn't much care about what made other people comfortable, she needed this job. So she merely shrugged her reply, which she figured was as close to the truth as she could get without alarming a stranger.

"Is there a problem here?" Stu asked as he appeared at her side.

Blake gestured to Black Bun, meaning *she* was the one causing the problem, but the woman clearly took it as Blake leaving it up to her to answer because she started in immediately. "This *person* you have working here doesn't know how to do her job."

Which was true. Blake couldn't really argue the point, but she couldn't help defending herself. "This lady invented a drink and expects us to make it."

The woman actually stomped her foot. "That is an outright lie. I get this drink here almost every day."

"And what is the drink, ma'am?" Stu asked.

"A grande quad nonfat one-pump no-whip mocha latte."

"Okay, no problem." He turned to one of the baristas behind them. "Maddie, can you make this woman's order?"

"Absolutely," Maddie said as she sprang into action.

Blake glared at Maddie, who'd clearly let Blake suffer through dealing with Black Bun when the girl had known the order the entire time. Silently, Blake put a voodoo curse on the pixie-haired traitor.

Stu told the woman her order would be comped, which caused her to flounce to the waiting area with her chin up. Blake extended the curse to include her too.

The next person in line was a guy with a much simpler order. Thank God. Blake made his coffee and rang him up with no issue. Soon after, Maddie rushed the woman's order over to her, and Black Bun disappeared into the crowd on the street.

Stu approached Blake a moment later. "Can I see you in my office?"

"You have an office?" The words were out of Blake's mouth before she had a chance to think about them first.

"Yes," Stu said slowly, suddenly looking at her as if she were something he needed to handle with extreme caution. "Gavin will take over for you until you come back."

Gavin materialized at her side, and Blake signed off the register so he could sign on. Then she followed Stu back to a small alcove he was incorrectly categorizing as an office. "Have a seat," he said as he pointed to an uncomfortable-looking plastic chair.

Against her better judgment, Blake sat. It was like sitting on a rock, which made her squirm. She had to make sure she focused on Stu instead of the sensation of sitting in a chair manufactured in hell.

Stu sat across from her in a rolling chair with a padded seat. Blake wanted to rip it out from beneath him and claim it for herself.

"So I see we need some more training," he said as he folded his hands on his desk.

"Yes. Training would be good," she replied, happy that it didn't seem like he was firing her.

"I'm a little surprised you need it. You said you had experience in coffeehouses before."

Blake rubbed her palms over her black yoga pants that had never seen a yoga class. "Yeah, I meant more along the lines of having gone into them rather than having worked in one."

Stu steepled his hands and rested the tip of his nose against his fingers. It was one of the grossest poses Blake had ever seen anyone strike. "I see," he said.

"I've worked on registers before." Which was true. "And I'm a fast learner." Which was a lie.

"Tell you what. I'm going to have you shadow Gavin for the rest of the day so you can get familiar with the orders. Then tomorrow, I'll have someone show you how to make them."

"Great," she said with a smile that was genuine for the first time that day. "I won't let you down." In reality she probably would, but she'd do her best to do a good job.

"Good to hear. I'll walk you out and tell Gavin the plan."

Blake nodded and hurriedly rose from the abominable chair. Following Stu, she tried to focus on not walking too closely behind. People got agitated when she did that.

"Gavin," Stu said when they got back to the counter. "Blake is going to shadow you for the rest of your shift to get more comfortable with our menu. That okay with you?"

"Sure," Gavin replied as he handed change back to an elderly man.

"Great. Good luck, Blake," Stu said before disappearing into the back.

Blake leaned against the counter and looked at Gavin since she'd only been able to shoot cursory glances at him before then. He was cute. Tall, blond, and broad. Though Blake was a bad judge of height at only five-two herself. But

Gavin seemed really big in every way. And he looked to be in his midtwenties, which would put him somewhere around her age. "You're hot," she blurted out.

Gavin looked over at her. "Thanks," he said casually. "You are too."

Blake looked down at herself. The best descriptor she could come up with was curvy. She was thin, but her boobs had started growing when she was eleven and never seemed to stop, which made her look a little heavier than she was. Not that she cared. It usually led to people being pleasantly surprised when they saw her naked.

She decided she wouldn't mind Gavin seeing her naked. "Do you have a girlfriend?"

Gavin rang up another customer and called out the order over his shoulder. "Nope."

"Boyfriend?"

"Nope."

Blake thought absently how she should be paying more attention to what Gavin was doing instead of how he looked, but looking at him was far more fascinating, especially now that he was this close to her.

"What about you?" he asked.

She was startled by his question, mostly because she'd started to mentally categorize him as more of a fantasy than an actual human and therefore hadn't expected him to ask questions. "What about me what?"

"Boyfriend? Or girlfriend?"

She hunched forward, dropping her arms onto the counter and resting on them. "Neither."

"Do you have a preference between the two?" he asked.

"Right now, my preference is decidedly male."

That earned her a small smile as he worked. Just then, Stu came out of the back and looked over at them. "Maybe you should pay attention to what I'm doing, and we can talk more about your preferences later," Gavin whispered.

Blake released a long sigh. "If we must," she said before she straightened up and tried her best to not press her boobs into Gavin while he worked.

CHAPTER TWO

"So he just left it like that? And you didn't make a concerted effort to strip down naked and demand he bang you like a prized stud horse?"

Blake moved her cell phone to her other ear as her best friend, Celeste, berated her for the missed opportunity. As if she hadn't been angry enough at herself. Gavin's shift had ended before hers, and he'd said a soft "Goodbye" before hurrying out the door. The only consolation she had was that Stu had tasked Gavin with helping her again the next day.

"As appealing as that image is, my manager was watching me like a hawk, and he's not my first choice for a threesome." Blake dumped spaghetti into a pot of water and turned on the burner. "But there's always tomorrow."

"Yeah. You better have a super-hot story to tell me tomorrow."

"I'll do my best."

"At least you still have a job. The manager could've fired you, and then you'd have lost the opportunity to have what I'm imagining will be a life-changing orgasm."

"Why are you imagining my orgasm?"

Celeste sighed. "Because I live a very sad life. So what's he look like? I need more specific details."

"My manager?"

"No. The guy you're seducing."

"I don't know that it counts as a seduction as much as a proposition."

"The end result is the same," Celeste argued.

"This is true. And I told you he's hot. Probably around six feet tall, short blond hair that's a little longer on top, wide like a football player, symmetrical features, green eyes."

"He sounds amazing in bed. Or on a table. Whatever surface is closest."

"You're nuts," Blake replied as she poured sauce into another pot she had on the stove.

"I'm aware. You working at the bar tonight?"

"Nah, I'm off because it was my first day at the coffeehouse, and I figured I'd be tired." Blake had been working at Reed's Bar for four years. She'd wandered in there after being fired from a clothing store nearby and had been hired after she'd broken up an almost bar fight by screaming, *Can you assholes move so I can get a drink?* Apparently being yelled at by a tiny white girl was somehow endearing. It was one of the few places where people seemed to like her as she was, and that made her love the place.

"Feel like grabbing dinner?" Celeste asked.

"I already started making something. Maybe another night."

"You're cooking?"

Blake went over to the refrigerator and took out the ketchup. "Yes, I'm cooking. Why?"

"You can't cook."

Sighing, Blake replied, "Everyone can cook, Celeste."

"What are you making?"

Blake was confused but thankful Celeste didn't continue arguing with her. "Spaghetti."

"What was that noise?"

"What noise?"

"That one. The one that sounds like you're squeezing a bottle."

Blake looked at the ketchup in her hand. "It's a bottle."

"Of what?" Celeste asked, her voice getting louder.

"Ketchup."

"Oh my God, Blake, are you putting ketchup on spaghetti?"

Blake scoffed. "Don't be ridiculous."

"Whew."

"I'm adding it to the sauce."

Celeste was silent for a moment, prompting Blake to look down at her phone to see if they'd been disconnected. "Why aren't you talking?"

"Because I don't know what to say."

"Okay. Do you want to call me back when you figure it out?" Blake offered.

"Why are you putting ketchup in your sauce?" Celeste asked, evidently having found her words.

"Because I didn't have enough sauce left, so I figured since they're both made from tomatoes, I could just combine them."

"How's that working out for you?"

"The consistency is weird. I think I need to add some water." Blake walked over to the sink and filled a cup.

"Please don't."

Blake poured the cup into the sauce and stirred.

"You did it, didn't you?" Celeste asked.

"Yup. It looks better."

"I feel bad for your kitchen."

Blake heard her front door unlock before it opened and closed. When she heard feet scuffle into the kitchen, she turned. "Hi, Bethany."

"Ugh, that bitch is home?" Celeste groaned through the phone.

Blake ignored the question and watched as her roommate, Bethany, walked to the refrigerator, flicking her long brown hair over her shoulder as she went.

"I'm making spaghetti if you want some," Blake offered.

Bethany peered into the fridge but must not have found anything worthwhile, because she came over to Blake and glanced into the pot. She immediately pulled back, her face pinched. "What the hell is that? It looks like blood."

Blake looked down into her sauce. "Oh, damn, you guessed the secret ingredient."

Bethany stared at her. "See. This is the shit that freaks me out. You're kidding, right?"

Blake just shrugged. If her roommate couldn't tell, why should Blake?

"I'm so over this crazy shit," Bethany muttered. She started to walk out of the kitchen before adding, "Oh, by the way, I'm moving out."

Blake's head snapped around in time to see a smirk on Bethany's lips.

"When?" Blake asked.

"Tomorrow," Bethany said in a sing-song voice that made Blake want to force-feed her an apple that would put her to sleep indefinitely. And with that, she stomped down the short hall and slammed her bedroom door.

"Well, she was pleasant as usual," Celeste said. "What'd she last? Two months?"

"Three," Blake replied as she stirred the spaghetti that looked wilted, but not in the way it was supposed to.

"Almost a record."

It was. The longest roommate Blake had ever had was Shelly at five months, and she'd only lasted as long as she did because she'd spent two of them hooked on keyboard duster and the remaining three in rehab.

"Maybe I should look for a male roommate next time. I get along great with all of the guys at Reed's."

Celeste laughed. "That's because you're hot, and they mistake your sarcasm for flirting."

"Are you hitting on me?"

"Jesus Christ. Throw that shitty dinner in the trash and meet me at Lobo's in half an hour. I don't want to give that asshole Bethany the satisfaction of finding you dead from food poisoning."

Blake turned off the stove and carried her sauce to the trash. "If you insist."

CHAPTER THREE

Gavin felt as though he was in perpetual motion. He ran from one job to the next to the next, and then home to sleep, only to wake up and do it all over again. As he raced down the street, he allowed himself to wallow in the misery that was his life. This wasn't the life he was meant to be living. But here he was, dealing with two jobs, one shittier than the next, just so he could keep a roof over his head. A roof that was being ripped away in a week.

A week. How the fuck was he going to find a place to live in a week? This was the problem with moving in with someone he met on Craigslist. There was a very real chance the roommate was using Gavin's rent money for PCP and prostitutes. The worst part was that Gavin should've known better. He should've insisted on being added to the lease and paying his share to the landlord directly. Instead, he'd allowed himself to be nothing more than a squatter in the dingy apartment of a pathological liar.

Gavin threw open the door to The Coffee Bean with more force than was necessary. He scanned the store, thankful it was mostly empty of customers. Then he looked behind the counter, and he was even more thankful. Blake was standing there tying the strings of her black apron around her small waist. It actually would've been difficult to tell just how thin she was if it weren't for the small pieces of fabric that cinched her shirt just under her chest.

Yesterday, Gavin had to force himself not to be a total perv and stare at her all day. Her terrific body, her wavy dark auburn hair that fell over her shoulders, her light-blue eyes, that smattering of freckles on her nose... She was beautiful. The fact that she seemed to have almost no filter was also attractive. Gavin had learned the hard way over the past few years that people rarely said what they meant or were honest about their intentions. In Gavin's world, Blake was a welcome anomaly.

"Hey, hotness," she shamelessly called out when she saw him.

He felt heat prick his face and couldn't help the shy smile that quirked his lips. Giving her a small wave, he dipped into the back to clock in and grab an apron. When he came back out front, tying his apron as he walked, he approached Blake. "Ready?" he asked.

"For...?"

He barked out a laugh, and damn did it feel good. He didn't laugh nearly enough anymore. "To learn how to make these drinks."

A look of disappointment crossed her features. "Oh. That's not nearly as fun as what I was thinking."

"I bet it wasn't." He shook his head at her brazenness even though he liked it.

He showed her where the recipe book was that she could reference if she got stuck. Then he explained the most common orders and a few variations of each.

"How does anyone remember all this?" she asked, her eyes wide.

Gavin shrugged. "Repetition. Most of these get ordered multiple times a day, so it becomes second nature. And the rare ones you can look up."

"I don't think my brain has room for all of this. I've been a bartender for four years, and I still don't remember how to make most of the drinks. I just throw whatever in a glass, and people know better than to complain."

He smiled again. "What happens if they complain?"

"I throw them out."

Eyebrows shooting up, Gavin said, "*You* throw people out?"

She widened her stance and put a hand on her hip. "What does that mean?"

"Can we pretend I never said that?"

Blake seemed to mull that over before dropping her arm. "Sure."

Gavin was dumbstruck for a second. "Wait. Really?"

Blake leaned a hip against the counter. "Yeah. I say shit I shouldn't all the time, so it'd be hypocritical of me to hold someone else accountable for the stupid things they blurt out."

Gavin thought there was an insult in there somewhere, but he didn't dwell on it. "Oh. Great. Thanks."

Blake nodded. "So let's talk about more interesting things."

"Like what?"

"Like you."

Trying to keep his face blank so she wouldn't pick up on just how much he *didn't* want to talk about himself, he asked, "What do you want to know?"

She tapped a finger against her chin for a few beats before answering. "Boxers or briefs?"

He rolled his eyes with a chuckle. When he saw her eyes alight with mischief, he decided she was teasing and didn't answer.

"Okay, a real question," she said. "How old are you?"

"Twenty-five," he answered.

"I'm twenty-six. I can be your sugar mama," she joked.

At least he thought she was joking. "Wouldn't be a hard position to qualify for," he said in an attempt to tease her back.

But her face grew serious, making it plain that he'd somehow missed the mark. She looked pensive as she studied him. "What qualifications would someone need? In case I find someone interested in applying."

Gavin laughed again, but it was humorless this time. "Right now, I'd settle for having a couch I could crash on." He wasn't sure why he was being so honest. He didn't need anyone knowing about his personal shit. But part of him wanted to get it off his chest, throw it out into the universe so he didn't have to carry it all on his own. Which was stupid, but he couldn't take it back now.

Blake's eyes grew wide as she bounced on her toes a little. "Oh my God, do you need a place to live? Say yes. Please, please, please say you're homeless."

Gavin had never seen someone so excited by the prospect of his homelessness. Even his parents hadn't seemed to take any actual joy in it, and they'd caused it in the first place.

He busied himself with restocking the cups as he answered. "Not yet. But in about a week I will be if I don't find something. But don't worry. I always land on my feet."

Blake grinned widely. "Well, it actually seems like you've landed right in my lap."

Gavin wasn't sure what that meant, but it sounded both dirty and promising.

◆ ◆ ◆ ◆

Blake couldn't believe her luck. Bethany's dad had shown up at the crack of dawn that morning to help her move her out. Luckily, most of the furniture was Blake's, since she was the constant in the apartment. Her roommates were the revolving door.

Bethany threw her things into garbage bags, and she and her dad carted them out and down the three flights of stairs without saying much of anything to Blake. Blake had nearly had to tackle Bethany to get the key to the apartment back. A key she'd shoved into her pocket and fingered now as she gazed excitedly at Gavin.

"Do I want to know what that means?" Gavin asked.

"I sure hope so." She clapped her hands. "This is so amazing. I'm really going to get to be a sugar mama. Though not really, because you'll need to pay rent. It's pretty cheap though. Four hundred a month. You're not going to find a better deal. So what do you say?"

Gavin's eyes narrowed. "Say to what?"

"Moving in with me! My roommate moved out this

morning, so you could move in immediately. She already paid for September, so you wouldn't even need to pay until October."

"You want me to move in with you?" he asked. He sounded confused, which she couldn't understand. She thought she was being pretty damn clear.

"Yes. It'll be perfect. I was just telling my friend Celeste how I should find a male roommate because the girls never last. And now here you are. It's like fate."

"Why do the girls not last?"

Uh-oh. This was exactly the kind of situation where Blake needed to slow down and think before she spoke. But she didn't. "Because I can be a little...much."

Gavin's eyes flashed with unease.

"But not like, serial-killer much," Blake added in a hurry. "I'm not hiding bodies in the floorboards or anything. But I am a tad eccentric. It becomes endearing after a while. You can ask my friend Celeste." Celeste had recommended Blake refer to herself as eccentric instead of saying she was "batshit crazy," which was off-putting. *Go figure.*

She eyed Gavin anxiously as he seemed to think over his options.

"So I could move in immediately?"

Trying to tamp down the flare of hope, she kept her voice even. "Yup."

Gavin thought for another moment before extending his hand in her direction. "Then you got yourself a roommate."

"Yay," she said as she ignored his hand and jumped into his arms for a hug.

"I have a feeling my life is about to get very interesting," he mumbled against her cheek.

She squeezed him tighter. "Probably. But in all the best ways."

CHAPTER FOUR

"Hey," Gavin said after letting himself into the apartment and walking toward Blake and Celeste who were sitting on Blake's couch. "Thanks for this."

"No problem," Blake said. When he'd texted to say he was downstairs, she'd unlocked the door and typed for him to come on in.

"Who is that?" Celeste whispered as she watched Gavin carry a large box to his bedroom.

He wore a fitted gray sleeveless shirt that showed off his biceps—and his pecs, Blake was certain, if he'd just put the damn box down. A few seconds later, he emerged from his bedroom, his arms hanging loosely at his sides—which allowed her to confirm her hypothesis about his chest—as he headed for the door.

"Oh. That was Gavin. He's moving in."

"You didn't tell me that." Celeste said it as though Blake had wronged her in some way.

"What are you talking about? I just told you."

Celeste rolled her eyes. "Is that, like, *The* Gavin?"

"Are there other Gavins I'm not aware of?" Blake said flatly.

Her comment earned her an elbow to her side from

Celeste. "Shut up. He's super hot. You were seriously gonna keep this a secret from me? You should be ashamed of yourself."

"I am. But not for that. I have other transgressions I'd rather not discuss."

Celeste narrowed her eyes at Blake like she wasn't sure whether there was truth to Blake's comment. Then her gaze darted to Gavin as he made another trip into his new room with a small TV and a few bags.

When he came out again, he flipped the white cap he was wearing backward. The action itself was hot, and it served to give a clearer view of his face, which Blake noticed had a gleam of sweat on it. His shirt was also damp, and when he brought the bottom up to wipe his face, Blake's gaze went to his abs. She was sure Celeste's had gone there too, though her friend no doubt made more of an effort to hide it.

"You need some help?" Blake asked. "The three-story walk-up is no joke in this heat."

"Yeah," Gavin said. "That'd be great! You sure you don't mind?"

"Oh. You want *us* to help. I meant more like calling some of your friends. But yeah, we can give you a hand, right, Celeste?"

Celeste looked as if Blake had volunteered her to participate in the Hunger Games. "I'll let you two have at it. I'm enjoying the view too much to trade it for hard labor."

Blake shrugged, not entirely bothered by the idea of spending some time with Gavin while sweat glistened on his muscles. "Suit yourself."

Gavin laughed softly before bringing a bottle of water up to his mouth and taking a long drink. The way his throat moved as he swallowed did things to Blake that made her wonder when Poland Spring had become an aphrodisiac. When he screwed the cap on and set it back down on the countertop, his gaze seemed to catch on the tile. She wasn't sure if it was the fact that it was only three-quarters finished or the theme that had caught his attention. He didn't comment on it, and Blake wondered if nothing about her could surprise him. "Thanks. I had two buddies who said they'd help but one's too hungover and the other's running late. He should get here soon though, so no worries if you don't wanna help. We'll get it done."

"Is he as sexy as you are?"

"Blake," Celeste scolded. "You know how I like to be surprised." Celeste turned to Gavin. "Just ignore her. She has a big mouth."

"You don't need to explain how I am," Blake said. "He already knows, and he's fine with it. Right, Gavin?"

Gavin's eyes had darted between the two women, but they settled back on Blake, the corner of his mouth rising in amusement. "Yup, it's all good."

"Then my question stands."

It seemed to take Gavin a moment to remember what the question had even been, but he didn't seem to mind answering once he did. "Yeah, uh, he's good-looking. I guess. I mean, I'm not gay or anything, so my opinion might not be the most accurate one, but—"

"Bullshit," Blake interrupted. "I hate when guys pretend they don't know if other guys are hot or not. Women can tell if other women are hot, and they have no problem stating it." She looked to Celeste, running her eyes over her friend's body.

Celeste squirmed in her seat at the appraisal, but that did nothing to deter Blake from sharing her judgment. "Celeste's a seven. An eight and a half when she puts on makeup and smiles."

Celeste punched her friend hard in the arm, but Blake had already prepared herself for what was coming and had pulled back in anticipation of the blow so that it barely grazed her. "I'm wearing makeup now," Celeste said.

"Oh. Then she's a six. Seven and a half at best." She laughed at Celeste's huff, but Blake knew she wasn't actually annoyed. Celeste was beautiful, more beautiful than Blake in Blake's opinion, and she'd told her friend that more times than she could remember. But she couldn't resist tormenting Celeste whenever she got the chance. Especially since Celeste never seemed to mind. "What do you think, Gavin?"

"Um... I don't...uh, can we go back to evaluating Simon?"

"His name's Simon?" Blake asked.

"Yeah, why?"

"It drops him down at least a half a point," she answered. "Simon's not a hot name."

"Agreed," Celeste said.

"Simon's a normal name," Gavin said in defense of his friend. "What's the matter with it?"

"It's one of the chipmunks," Blake countered.

"Oh, and that old English guy who used to be on *American Idol.*"

"Yes," Blake said. "This game's fun. Let me think."

Blake wondered if Gavin would join in, but he seemed too busy trying to figure out what the hell was wrong with them to actually take part in the game.

"Oh, I got another one!" Celeste said. "Simon's the name of Farrah's boyfriend. Although I guess they aren't together anymore, so he's not technically her boyfriend."

This time Blake looked as confused as Gavin did. "Who the hell are you talking about?" she asked.

"From *Teen Mom*. Farrah," she said as if repeating the name would cause Blake and Gavin to recall a person they didn't know about. "She was the one who had that anal porn video."

Blake raised her eyebrows. "Still don't know who you're talking about, but now I'm intrigued."

"Was the tape with the Simon guy?" Gavin asked.

"No. Someone else."

"I don't..." Gavin narrowed his eyes as he seemingly tried to figure out what Celeste was talking about. "Would he be hotter if he *was* the ass porn guy?"

"That," Blake said, pointing at Gavin, "is an excellent question."

"No, because Farrah's a slutty asshole, and anyone who willingly associates with her must therefore also be a slutty asshole. He thinks he's hot shit, and she's annoying and fake." She crossed her arms like her explanation had made all the sense in the world. "It's the law of transference."

"Yeah, I don't know what that is," Gavin said.

"Me either," Blake agreed. "I lost you at 'slutty asshole.'"

Their conversation was interrupted by a knock at the open door, and a man with floppy, dark hair stepped inside carrying a box. "I'm not sure what I'm walking into, but I'm assuming I have the right place." He looked at Gavin, who was laughing hysterically.

Celeste huffed. "Never mind. My theory's blown anyway. He's hot." She thrust an arm in Simon's direction as if the realization disappointed her.

"Hi," Simon said, shifting the box to one arm so he could extend the other as he headed to the couch to greet Celeste and Blake. It made the muscles in his left arm even more defined than they already were. "I'm Simon."

"We know," Blake said, giving his hand a gentle shake.

"That's Blake, and I'm Celeste." Celeste's words sounded almost like a song, and it made Blake roll her eyes. "It's a pleasure to meet you."

"It's a pleasure to meet you too, Celeste." Then he added, "Like the pizza, right?" as if the connection with the frozen meal would somehow make it more likely that he'd remember her name.

Blake didn't think Simon had meant the comment as an insult. The opposite actually. He didn't seem like the sharpest tool in the shed and struck her as the type who probably enjoyed a frozen pizza from time to time. He'd probably meant it as a compliment.

"Um...yeah, I guess," Celeste said, causing Simon to smile and reveal two dimples.

On Celeste's suggestion, she and Blake heated up some popcorn and watched the guys carry some furniture and a few more boxes up for the next half hour or so. When they were just about done, Simon wiped the sweat from his brow with the top of his shirt.

"I'm an awful hostess," Blake said. "I should have offered you some lemonade or something."

"Thanks. Lemonade would be great," Simon replied.

"Oh. I actually don't think I have any," Blake clarified. "It was more of an expression."

"Offering lemonade to someone is an expression?" Simon asked.

"Maybe 'expression' wasn't the right word. I meant..." Blake sighed, unable to explain herself. "I have cold drinks I'm happy to offer you, but not lemonade."

"Oh, okay. Anything's fine," Simon answered.

Blake got up and headed into the kitchen. "I've got water...from the tap, of course, because who willingly pays for something they can get for free, right?" Blake asked though she didn't expect a reply. "And I think we have a few beers left." She opened the fridge. "Yeah, some beer and some kind of V8 drink my old roommate left in there. But I'm pretty sure only whackjobs drink vegetables, so I'm sure you don't want that."

"Um, no, probably not. I'll take a beer for the road if you have one."

Blake wondered if Simon actually planned to drink his beer *while* driving, but she decided she'd rather not know. Instead, she pulled out four beers and passed one to each of them.

"To my adventures with my new roommate," Gavin said, raising his bottle for the others to follow.

"More like *mis*adventures," Celeste said.

Blake held hers up again as she smiled at Gavin. "Okay, then. Here's to many misadventures with my new roommate."

Then she clinked bottles with the other three, thinking that was definitely a toast she could get on board with.

◆ ◆ ◆ ◆

Gavin finished unpacking the last of his clothes and made his way back out to the small living room. If it could even be called that. The space looked more like a strange antique shop you might find in some sort of coastal town. Strange trinkets, like an elephant made out of blue glass and an old rotary phone— which he was certain didn't work since it wasn't plugged into the wall—were lined up neatly on some of the wooden shelves along the perimeter of the room.

He was thankful he'd warned Simon before he'd come over not to comment on anything. By Blake's own admission, she was a bit strange, and Gavin didn't know what they'd be walking into that morning when he moved his stuff in.

But as he took the time to look at what would now be considered his home, he realized how accurate his prediction had been. The space was a hodgepodge of eclectic furniture: two mustard-yellow pleather-covered barstools in the dining area, a worn couch that looked like it'd been upholstered with red-and-black shirts from a lumberjack's closet, and an assortment of small, mismatched tables that were sprinkled around without—in Gavin's opinion—much of a purpose.

Most of them were completely bare, except for a few empty soda cans, which appeared to have been discarded there while Blake had been passing through the space. Why she hadn't bothered to walk the additional seven or so steps to the kitchen to throw them out would probably remain one of the many mysteries about the woman. Another mystery was why she'd chosen to retile part of the kitchen counter.

Herself.

He'd *assumed* she'd done it herself anyway. Gavin couldn't imagine that she would've had the money to hire someone to do it, nor did he think a professional would have done work that looked like what was in front of him. He'd first noticed the odd choice in tile earlier in the day when he was talking to Blake and Celeste but had decided not to ask Blake why she'd chosen to decorate a place where people ate with tiles depicting silhouettes of people posing in various Kama Sutra positions. The fact that he found himself hoping she planned to finish the remaining few square feet alarmed him slightly.

As someone whose passion consisted of portraying scenes and people in the most beautiful way possible, Gavin found himself almost confused by his new environment. No lighting or camera angle could make this setting pleasing to the eye. At least, he didn't think so. The walls of the entire apartment, including his new bedroom, were painted a pale coral, which only made the apartment that much more aesthetically unappealing. It didn't strike him as a place someone would necessarily want to live. But here he was, about to do just that with a semi-stranger. He picked up his camera from the coffee table and snapped a few pictures of the strange decor. He wasn't sure why he wanted to document a place he wasn't sure he even wanted to be, but there he was. After taking a close-up of the tiles, Gavin put his camera down.

"Fuck," he breathed out as he ran a hand through his curly blond hair. "What am I doing here?"

"I don't know," a voice said dryly from behind him. "Talking to yourself?"

"Shit," Gavin said with a jolt as he spun around to see Blake, who was now wearing some sort of top that barely came below her breasts. "I didn't realize you were still here."

"That's what made me say you were talking to yourself."

"Yeah...um...I'm just a little overwhelmed at the moment. It'll pass."

He thought he saw a hint of a smile, but it almost seemed like she'd decided not to follow through with it. "I have that effect on people."

Gavin chose to ignore her comment, which left them looking at one another in awkward silence.

"What were you taking pictures of?" she finally asked.

Gavin looked over at his camera as if it was going to answer for him. "Oh, uh, nothing really. It's just something I do. Take pictures, I mean. I'm a photographer." Which was a stupid thing to explain because he'd already told her about his other job one day at the coffee shop.

She took a step toward him. "Can I see?"

"Um..." Gavin hesitated. While people obviously saw the pictures he took for work at the portrait studio, he hadn't shown anyone his personal photos in a long time. But unsure how to refuse, Gavin picked up his camera and turned it back on before handing it to her so she could see the screen.

He watched her click through the photos, mostly candids he'd taken as he wandered around the city. She was silent as she scrolled, which made him anxious. After a few minutes, she lowered the camera. "These are incredible."

Gavin shrugged. "They're okay. I could do better if I concentrated more, but I mostly just take them for fun."

"Well, I think they're pretty damn good."

"Thank you." He felt a blush creeping up his neck, so he changed the subject by asking her what she'd been up to the past few hours because he hadn't heard her in a while.

"Sleeping," she said simply. "But Guy and Baby woke me up."

"Who?" Gavin wasn't sure he even wanted to know who Blake was talking about, but he found himself asking anyway.

She gestured toward her room with a nod. "The neighbors on that side of the apartment. They only know how to do two things—fight and fuck," she explained.

"And their names are Baby and Guy?"

"No. I don't know what their names are. The guy's always calling the girl baby, and she never says his name at all. And since I don't care enough to ask them, I guess I'll never know."

Gavin laughed. "Oh. So what is it this time?"

"What is what?" Blake asked, confused.

"What are they doing? Fighting or fucking?"

"Oh. Fighting. Or they were when I came out here, but sometimes one leads to the other, so who knows what they're up to now."

"Interesting," Gavin said with an amused smile. "Guess it's good my room's on the other side of the apartment then."

Blake shrugged. "Depends on which you prefer. I'm pretty sure your dude's birth records are written on parchment paper with a quill somewhere. He watches reruns of *MacGyver* at a decibel level that would rival most military-grade helicopters."

"Shit," Gavin said. "I think I'd prefer your couple. I feel like there's a level of entertainment to them that I won't get with Richard Dean Anderson."

"Probably. Sometimes when Baby gets exceptionally emotional, she starts yelling at him in another language. I don't even think he understands what she's saying," Blake told him with a smile. "You wanna come listen?"

"To Guy and Baby?" Gavin raised an eyebrow. "Fuck yeah, I do. Do you ever bang on the wall or tell them to shut up or anything?" he asked as they walked down the short hall to Blake's room.

"I did when I first moved in, but it only encourages them to be louder. Now I usually put on headphones or something if it's the middle of the night."

Gavin nodded, thinking that he needed to make sure he looked for his earbuds. He didn't remember unpacking them, and he had a habit of constantly losing them. "You weren't kidding. They really *are* loud," he said as soon as he was in Blake's room. With her door shut, he hadn't even heard them. But now that there was only a thin piece of drywall between him and the Odd Couple, he had no trouble hearing every word.

"Because that's the jelly I like, that's why!" yelled a female voice. "You'll eat the grape. I won't. So stick to that instead of using all of mine."

"Come on, baby. You're making a big deal out of nothing."

"Am I?" she spat. "Speaking of nothing, that's what I'll be having for breakfast tomorrow now that I don't have anything to put on my English muffin."

Gavin was puzzled. "They're really fighting about jelly?"

"Not when I left, they weren't. Guy was telling her he was going bowling with the guys."

"Guy has guys?" Gavin asked, amused with his own joke.

"Guess so. Baby said he was just out last night and she wanted to spend time together. I think that's why she starts the fights to begin with. Like she's looking for a way to interact with him or something."

"That's...insightful," Gavin said before adding, "but also a little disturbing. Isn't that what kids do? Like when toddlers throw tantrums?"

"I wouldn't know. I'm not much of a kid person."

Gavin had the urge to ask her what that meant exactly, but it occurred to him that it wasn't his business. Blake seemed like a private person, and Gavin didn't want to pry.

Blake's eyes remained on the wall, and Gavin noticed that her room was the only one in the apartment that wasn't painted a muted coral. Three walls were a pale blue, but the one they were currently looking at was white. Or had been at one time. Now it was more of a dark eggshell that had been marred with scratches and stray smudges. From what, Gavin wasn't sure.

He wondered why she'd chosen to leave that wall so plain when the rest of the apartment was in such sharp contrast to it. And though he didn't know for sure that she'd even been the one to choose the colors, something told him she was.

The two of them stayed silent for a few minutes as they stared at the scarred wall, watching a show that neither of them could see.

"What do you want me to do?" Guy asked. "I'll stop on

39

the way home and get more strawberry jelly if that's what you want. But there's still some in here. Look."

There was a lull in the conversation before Baby spoke again. "Jesus, this isn't about the jelly." The sound of glass shattering made both Blake and Gavin jolt in response, but neither of them looked at the other.

"Maybe his name's Jesus," Gavin said, turning his head toward Blake.

She returned his stare, tearing her gaze from the wall to look at him. "What?"

"Guy's name," he said. "Baby called him 'Jesus.'"

"She didn't *call* him Jesus. She was using it as an expletive," Blake argued.

"Do you know that for sure?" Gavin asked, knowing that his suggestion was a ridiculous one.

Blake rolled her eyes. "I'm like ninety-nine-point-nine percent sure that people with that name don't pronounce it with the hard *J*."

"Well, there are like seven billion people in the world, so if one-tenth of a percent of them pronounce it that way, that's like"—Gavin paused as he tried to do the math, but that only resulted in Blake looking more amused, and this time it was at his expense—"I don't know, like millions of people or something. There are probably hard *J* Jesuses everywhere that we haven't heard of."

"Jesuses?" Blake repeated.

"Yeah. Jesuses. What do you think the plural would be? Like Jesi or something?"

Blake shook her head at him. "You might be even weirder

than I am, and that makes me much more confident that this new living arrangement is going to work out just fine." Without waiting for a reply she headed back out the door, leaving Gavin in her room alone to wonder just how weird his new roommate actually was.

CHAPTER FIVE

"We should probably talk about the rent," Gavin said.

"What about it?" Blake asked. When she'd offered him the room a few days ago, she'd told Gavin how much it would be, and he'd happily agreed, especially since he wouldn't have to pay until the following month. He said it was less than he'd been paying at his old place, and since he didn't have any other options, he didn't try to negotiate the price with her. "If you were thinking of paying me in sexual favors instead of cash, you should know that I'm broke. So as much as I'd like to agree to those terms, my bank account won't let me."

Gavin chuckled, taking a seat next to her on the plaid couch. He rubbed his hands over his thighs like he wasn't sure he wanted to say whatever he'd been thinking.

"Gavin, please don't tell me the rent's too much now that you've already moved in. As much as I love your body, I have no problem inflicting some serious injuries to it if I need to."

"No. No," Gavin said. "The rent's fine. But I wanted to talk about getting my name added to the lease if possible. It's why I lost my other place. I was giving my roommate money and assuming he was using it to pay the rent. But then our landlord evicted us. Or *him*, I guess would be more accurate, because his name was the only one on any of the paperwork. I found out he had a bad drug habit, and that's where all my money was going." He looked up from where his stare had been fixated on a gray spot on the carpet. "I know it's a shitty thing to ask because you seem nice and...*not* at all like a drug addict—"

"Whoa, slow down with the compliments, Casanova. You're gonna make a girl blush."

Gavin laughed, but Blake could tell it was out of embarrassment. It was cute. "Sorry. I didn't mean that... It's just that we don't really know each other well, other than as coworkers, and since I got royally screwed over the last time, I need to make sure I protect myself. It's nothing against *you*. I'd do this with anyone."

"Would it make you feel better if I showed you my boobs?"

Gavin's eyes widened. "What? Why would you want to—"

Blake shrugged. "You said we didn't know each other well, so I figured it'd be a good way to begin to open up. Like an icebreaker of sorts," she explained.

"Are you serious?" Gavin asked, clearly shocked by her offer. "You wanna get to know each other by stripping?"

"The thought may have crossed my mind on more than one occasion," Blake said. "Oh, and to answer your question about getting your name on the lease, that's totally fine. I completely get not wanting to trust someone you barely know. Although, it usually works the opposite way with me. The more I get to know someone, the less I trust them."

"Really?" She could see the concern in his eyes, like he wanted her to elaborate but thought he probably shouldn't ask her to. She was thankful for it.

"Yeah. People suck," she answered casually. "In my

experience anyway." There was a moment between them where neither spoke, and all that could be heard was the buzz of the refrigerator. "But," she said, trying to keep her voice light, "if you still wanna see my boobs, I'm totally game."

Gavin coughed out a laugh. "You're one of a kind, you know that?"

An amused smile crept over Blake's face at his comment. "Yup," she said with a nod.

♦ ♦ ♦ ♦

"Oh my God," Celeste said. "You're totally gonna bang him. I know it. I can't believe you haven't already."

"You don't *know* anything," Blake argued.

"Oh, I know this. His penis," she said slowly as she inserted a finger through the fist of her other hand for effect, "is going to be in your vagina before the end of the week. I bet you five dollars."

"You're betting on my sex life?" Blake asked.

"It appears I am, yes. But my own life is clearly even sadder than we both originally thought, so I need to live vicariously."

"He wouldn't even look at my boobs. I mean seriously, what guy turns down an offer like that?"

"A sweet one," Celeste replied.

Blake gave her friend an exaggerated laugh. "That means nothing. Even sweet guys are horny. There's no logical explanation for why he wouldn't want to see them other than the hypothesis I just now came up with."

"Which is what? He's gay?" Celeste grabbed Blake's arm. "Please don't tell me he's gay! That'll be devastating."

"He's not gay," Blake assured her. "I already asked him that the first day I had to shadow him at work."

"Oh. Good," Celeste said, releasing her grip on Blake's forearm. "Then what's your explanation for it?"

Blake leaned back in her chair and stared out the window of the deli in sadness. "That he has a tiny dick."

"What?" Celeste popped a potato chip into her mouth and took a sip of her soda. "That makes no sense."

"It's the *only* thing that makes sense," Blake said, turning back to her friend. "Hear me out. He probably felt like if I showed him mine, he'd have to show me his. Otherwise he'd seem like a total perv who just wants to look at women's boobs all day."

"But that was your offer," Celeste said.

"I know. But still. I think he would've felt obligated to return the favor. Or at least *offer* to. What other reason would he have to not want to show me? It's gotta be small. Like microscopic, Celeste. Because guys show their junk to anybody who wants to look. And also to anybody who doesn't wanna look," she added as an afterthought. "Remember that guy on the subway who kept flashing people but claimed it wasn't indecent exposure because he had it covered with a banana peel?"

Celeste sighed in what Blake identified as defeat. "As much as it pains me to admit it, you might be onto something here."

"Thank you," Blake said, pleased with herself.

"But that could just mean that he didn't want you to see his little man in the light. You know...where you could evaluate its size and shape and all that. That logic doesn't transfer to fucking. All guys fuck if they get the opportunity. Doesn't matter what they look like or how minuscule their dongs are. If someone offers to fuck them, they fuck. Besides, maybe he grows more than shows."

"Maybe you're right," Blake admitted.

"Of course I'm right," Celeste said. "Every guy fucks."

Blake took a look around the diner at the people surrounding them. "Okay," Blake said. "I'm choosing to believe you only because believing you results in me having sex with Gavin. Who I'm still imagining has a huge cock until I find out otherwise."

"Good," Celeste said. "I'm glad that's settled."

"Me too," said a partially balding man who'd been sitting on the other side of Celeste at the counter. Blake hadn't even noticed him until he'd spoken. His rounded shoulders made him look...puffy, and his voice didn't sound much deeper than her own. He reminded Blake of someone who might've worked on Best Buy's Geek Squad. "But if it doesn't work out with this Gavin guy," he said, "give me a call." Then he stood, and on the way to throw out his trash, he slipped Blake his number on a napkin and added, "Because I fuck too."

Blake picked up the napkin at the corner with two fingers like it might have been laced with some sort of drug that would result in her winding up in the trunk of a car with no recollection of how she got there.

"At least now you have a Plan B," Celeste said, causing them both to burst out into fits of laughter.

CHAPTER SIX

Gavin had been at the coffeehouse for three hours, but it felt like a lot more. Maybe it was that it was during the weekday lull between rush hour and lunchtime—when people were still happily caffeinated from their morning fix and didn't feel the need to come in until they started fiending for their afternoon pick-me-up. But he'd been working there long enough to be used to the boredom and usually had no problem busying himself with any task he could find: restocking paper products, taking out the trash, doing inventory. He didn't even mind cleaning bathrooms if it helped pass the time.

But today he'd done all those things only to find his mind wishing away the hours like a bad herpes outbreak. Not that he'd know what that felt like.

It wasn't until ten o'clock when Gavin realized the reason for his urge to speed up time. And that reason was barely over five feet tall and had just walked in wearing a shirt that said Caffeine and Cardio. It occurred to Gavin that he didn't think Blake even worked out, at least not that he'd seen in the few days they'd been living together. Not that she needed to.

"You're late."

Gavin looked up from where he'd been filling the straws to see Stu standing at the counter, his hands on his hips as he stared at Blake.

"Am I?"

"You are. Three minutes to be exact."

"Sorry," Blake said, and Gavin could tell she was doing her best to seem contrite. Her eyes locked on his for a moment, and she gave him a quick smile before looking back at Stu. "Won't let it happen again."

Stu nodded before pointing out that the other thing she wouldn't let happen again was wearing a tank top to work.

"Seriously?" Blake glanced down at her shirt. "It says 'Caffeine' though. This is a coffee shop. I'm practically a mascot for the place today. You should be giving me a raise, not reprimanding me."

Gavin tried to hide his laugh.

"Shirts without sleeves are out of dress code," Stu said.

"Oh. Is this in a manual somewhere or something?" Blake asked.

"Yes. It's in the one I gave you when I hired you, but I'm guessing you didn't read it. You can take one of the shirts we sell, and I'll just take the money for it out of your paycheck."

"'Kay," Blake said with a sigh before putting her bag under the cabinet below the counter and heading over to the wooden shelving unit that housed the coffee shop's apparel.

Gavin walked over and stood next to her. "Sup?" he said before he could stop himself from asking something so dumb.

"Oh, nothin' much," Blake answered. "Just trying to choose which thirty-two-dollar T-shirt I'd like to buy."

Gavin put his hands in his pockets and looked at the selection. "I say get the blue. Can't go wrong with a color that matches your eyes," he said.

"I thought I couldn't go wrong with a shirt that advertised caffeine either, but now I'm paying thirty-two dollars for it."

Gavin turned away from the clothing to face her. "Well, if it helps, I like it." He wanted to tell her that one of the reasons he liked it was that the words drew more attention to her chest without making him seem like a complete perv for looking at it. A chest that he'd, by some miracle, been able to decline seeing when she'd offered a few nights ago. He hadn't wanted to seem like some middle school boy who jumped at the chance to see some girl's tits. But he'd be kidding himself if he pretended he wasn't interested. And not only in Blake's body. But in her. She was funny and confident and open. Yet she also had a sort of mystery about her that made Gavin want to see what made her tick.

"Thanks," she said with a small smile before reaching for a small baby-blue T-shirt.

"Oh wait," Gavin said, holding up a finger and already walking backward as he spoke. "I just remembered I have an extra T-shirt in my car."

"Oh my God, Gavin. You're a lifesaver," she called as he exited the store.

He tried not to think dirty thoughts about what it was like to hear Blake say, "Oh my God, Gavin," but he couldn't help it. She was cute and seemed to be more comfortable with her sexuality than most of the women he'd been around. Gavin grabbed the shirt from his bag and shut the trunk of his car. When he got back inside, she was coming back from clocking in. "Here you go," he said, handing her the shirt. "Sorry. It's a little big." He held up the red shirt to her torso and saw that it came down to her midthigh. "Or maybe a lot big."

She looked down. "But it also has a heart on it and says, 'I tolerate you.'" She gave him a warm smile. "It's perfect."

A few minutes later, she came out of the bathroom with her sleeves rolled and the bottom of her shirt tied to the side so it fit snugly around her waist. "Do you care that I tied it like this?" she asked. "It might stretch it."

"Nope. I've only worn it like one time or something. I keep it in the car for emergencies."

Blake laughed. "Are there lots of T-shirt emergencies?"

Gavin rubbed the back of his neck. "I guess only ones when pretty roommates choose the wrong outfit for their shift."

Blake smiled at him, but her gaze dropped away from his for a moment. "Well, thanks. For the shirt *and* the compliment," she said.

"My pleasure. Glad it went to good use. My college roommate gave it to me as a joke at the end of our freshman year."

"You went to college?" Blake asked, and Gavin didn't know whether to be offended that she couldn't believe he'd attended any type of higher education or flattered that he didn't seem like the type to.

"Went, yes. Graduated, no," he clarified.

Blake grabbed an apron from behind the counter and tied it around her waist. "Why?"

"Why did I go, or why didn't I graduate?"

She thought for a moment. "Both."

Gavin shrugged. It was a complicated answer, but he

chose to make it as simple as possible. "I went because that's what my parents expected me to do, and I dropped out because I shouldn't have ever gone to begin with."

"Shit, really? Were your parents pissed?"

"Pissed would probably be an understatement," he said. He noticed a customer walk up to the counter and look at the menu board. He gave a nod toward the woman so Blake saw her too, and then they both headed over. Though Blake had picked up on mostly everything once she'd given it a little effort, she continued to shadow Gavin as Stu had asked her to. And Gavin was happy to have the company.

"What can we get for you?" Blake asked the woman.

"I'm not sure," she said. She looked to be about the same age and size as Blake but seemed to be her opposite in every other way. The girl looked like she smiled all the time, which highlighted the freckles sprinkled over her cheekbones, and her strawberry-blond hair was pulled up into a high ponytail. Something told him Blake would never be caught dead in a high ponytail. "What would you recommend?" Her question was clearly directed at Gavin and was said in such a bubbly voice he almost laughed.

"Um, I don't know." It wasn't that he'd never been asked for a recommendation before, and he was comfortable giving them. But most of the time when someone asked the barista for a suggestion, the person gave some sort of indication as to what they were looking for—an afternoon boost that wasn't too heavy or some sort of cold coffee with a hint of sweetness. "Were you thinking of getting coffee or something else?"

"Either," she answered. "But I don't want something that's

too high in calories." Somehow she managed to smile even wider, and Gavin could've sworn he saw her bat her eyelashes more times than were probably necessary. "Don't want to lose my bikini body." She laughed at her own comment.

"Have you tried the sweet cream cold brew?" Blake asked. "You can add a flavor to it. Vanilla, mocha, caramel, whatever you like."

Gavin hadn't expected Blake to suggest a drink, but now that she had, he knew why. Their sweet cream cold brew was high in fat and not exactly light on calories, especially if the woman chose to add some sort of flavored syrup to it.

"I haven't," the customer said. "Do *you* like it?" she asked Gavin.

Gavin looked to Blake, who was leaning her head in her palm as she rested her elbow on the high countertop nearby. "Yeah, Gavin. What do you think? Should she get the sweet cream cold brew?"

Blake's devious smile made Gavin turn up a side of his lip as well. "Yeah, it's good," he said once his gaze had returned to the woman in front of him. "I like it with vanilla and caramel."

"That sounds good," she said. "I'll take a medium one of those. My name's Sami, by the way."

"Oh," Gavin said as he rung her up. "We don't take names here. We just go by the number on your receipt. And that'll be four nineteen."

She slid her card through the reader and punched in her code.

Gavin handed her the receipt and told her it would be ready in a minute and delivered at the other end of the counter.

A few minutes later, Gavin handed the woman her drink, and she left, telling him she'd see him later. He wasn't sure if that was a polite goodbye or a literal statement of her intentions, but he tried not to think about it.

Once the woman was gone, Blake spoke. "Nice one recommending two flavors instead of one. I'm impressed. I didn't think you had it in ya."

"You guys are horrible," Maddie said before Gavin had the chance to reply. He hadn't even realized she'd been behind the counter.

Gavin kind of agreed with her, but Blake was quick to defend them. "Why? That kind woman asked for a drink recommendation, so we suggested one. We were being helpful."

Maddie scoffed. "Please. You told her to get something that has like four hundred calories in it when she told you she was watching her caloric intake."

Blake squared her shoulders at Maddie and crossed her arms. "Well, the lie detector determined *that* was a lie."

Gavin laughed at the allusion to *Maury*, but the joke had clearly missed its mark on Maddie, who looked puzzled. "What are you talking about? What lie detector?"

Blake shook her head. "Never mind. I meant I know she was lying about counting calories. She has a great body, and anyone who's truly counting calories would've known that drink had a shit ton of them in there, even if she didn't know the exact number. She'll be fine."

"You can't mess with a customer like that just because she had a thing for Gavin. It's wrong. And if you do it again, I'm telling Stu."

"Snitches get stitches," Blake said.

"Clever saying. Did you make that up?"

Blake stared at her for a moment before saying, "I didn't come up with it. Jesus. You're not even any fun to threaten."

"Wait, you're threatening me?" Maddie asked.

"Why? You gonna tell Stu if I am?" Blake glared, and Gavin sensed the shift in her. The imposing presence that made her intimidating despite her small stature.

Blake's glare seemed to make Maddie think about her response. "Let's all just get back to work," she said before turning and walking toward the Keurig cups to continue stocking them.

◆ ◆ ◆ ◆

"I think you might've actually scared her at the end there," Gavin said once Maddie was far enough away from them that she couldn't hear.

Blake looked over at her. "You think? She's like five-foot-ten and probably has thirty pounds on me. Besides, I doubt she thought I would actually hit her or anything."

"You wouldn't?" Gavin asked, his eyebrow raised like he didn't believe her for a second.

"Of course not. I'm trying to keep this job, not lose it. I was intentionally vague for a reason."

"You told her 'Snitches get stitches,'" he said with a laugh.

It was a valid point. "That's true. But people can end up with stitches for a number of reasons that don't include me punching her."

"Like...?" he asked, drawing out the word as a way of

proving his point.

"I don't know," Blake said. "Like...getting their wisdom teeth taken out?"

"You're going to remove Maddie's wisdom teeth if she tells on you?"

His comment made Blake laugh out loud. "Okay, I admit that sounds strange. Maybe she'll trip on her way out of Stu's office and bite her tongue. They'll have to stitch it back together, but it'll still keep her from ever talking again."

Gavin leaned against the counter and put his hands on the edge, making his biceps somehow fill the sleeves of his black T-shirt a bit more than they did already. He cocked his head to the side, clearly amused. "Oh, okay. That's much more plausible. So Karma is the one giving her the stitches, not you."

"Exactly," Blake said with a smile. "Karma's the bitch, not me."

Gavin nodded before pushing off the counter. "I totally get it now. And speaking of Stu, we better get back to work. He'll have our asses if he sees us standing around like this."

"'Kay," Blake said. "I definitely don't want anyone else having your ass before I get to." She walked around to the other side of the counter and began to innocently look through the packaging dates of some of the cookies and muffins.

"You want my ass?" Gavin asked, but Blake did her best to keep a straight face without looking up.

She took a few more cellophane-wrapped cookies out of the basket and set them aside. "Do we just throw these away after forty-eight hours?" she asked, holding up an oatmeal raisin.

"Yes," he answered. And then, "What were you thinking of doing with it?"

"I'm sure there are homeless shelters that would love to have some."

"Of my ass?" he asked, and this time, Blake's head popped up in surprise.

"No, not your ass! This food! Why would homeless people want some of your ass?"

"They wouldn't. That's why...I was wondering what you..." Gavin couldn't seem to finish a cohesive thought. Instead he rubbed his hand through his hair in a way that resembled a confused puppy. It was fun to watch. Finally he sighed as he seemed to get his thoughts together. "You said that Stu better not have my ass before you, and then you started talking about cookies, but I wasn't talking about cookies. I was still talking about my ass, and...I know that sounds weird," he said with a shake of his head. "And now I'm rambling and... Jesus, it was just an odd thing to say, I guess. That you wanted my ass, so I was asking what you wanted to do with it."

Blake remained stoic, enjoying how flustered the gorgeous man in front of her got at the mention of his ass. But after a few moments, she couldn't help but let out the small laugh she'd been holding in.

"Great, you're laughing at me now. I feel so much better," he said with a shake of his head. "Are you purposely messing with me?"

"Possibly. It's so much fun," she answered. "But I *was* serious about wanting your ass. And to answer your question— because I know guys can be quite protective of that area—I wasn't thinking of doing anything weird to it. I'm only interested in seeing it." She paused for a moment before adding, "Okay, full disclosure... I'm also probably interested in grabbing it."

Her last sentence caused Gavin to choke on the air he'd breathed in.

"I wasn't planning on jamming anything into it, so no worries there," she continued while he struggled to collect himself. Holding up her right hand, she said, "Scout's honor."

Finally Gavin seemed to relax enough to pull in a deep breath so that he could speak. "Okay. Well, that's good to know," he said. "About the not-jamming-things-in-there part, because I'm not sure I'd be into that."

She stared at him for a moment, her eyes overtly raking over him in a way that she was sure he'd picked up on. His body was so rigid, and his gaze was so fixated on her face that she guessed he was struggling to keep it there. Finally, her eyes landed back on his. "So that means you're into the rest of it?" she asked.

His face remained expressionless for a moment before the corners of his lips raised into a small smile. "I might be," he said before turning away from her and walking into the back room.

His words sounded like a challenge. And Blake loved a good challenge.

CHAPTER SEVEN

Blake wiped a hand through the condensation on the bathroom mirror and looked at her reflection. She scrunched up her hair with her hands and lightly slapped her cheeks to give them some more color, even though she was already a bit flushed from her shower. Giving herself a seductive look, she steeled herself to see her plan through.

She'd left Gavin in the living room where they'd been watching TV. *Life in the ER* had never been so titillating. The sexual tension, which seemed to only affect Blake since Gavin had looked as relaxed as she'd ever seen him, had almost made her throw herself across his lap and beg him to fuck her with his maybe-big-but-more-likely-small dick. Gavin had been living with her for almost a week, and Celeste's prediction had yet to come to fruition. Even though its occurrence would cost Blake five dollars, she'd decided that it was a bet she'd gladly lose.

But Gavin had seemed to solidly friend-zone her, which wasn't a place she could remember ever being. It was a desolate, horrifying place, and she wanted out of there stat. Hence the impromptu shower. Blake figured wrapping a small towel around her wet, naked body would get things progressing in the right direction.

There was a quiet and annoying voice in the back of her head that said banging her roommate was not a smart move. She did genuinely like living with Gavin, which was a big change for her. And even stranger, he seemed to like living with *her*. She knew sex could make things complicated. Blake suddenly wished she'd banged one of her previous roommates so she had a frame of reference. Currently, it didn't even matter to her that they'd all been females. She'd do almost anything in the name of science, and that would've been one experiment she would've given her left breast to have conducted. Well, maybe not the left one. That one was her favorite.

Mind made up, she tucked her towel around herself a little tighter in the hopes that her boobs would bust it open at precisely the right moment. Then she pulled open the door and walked down the hallway toward the kitchen. She tried to get a quick peek at Gavin when she walked between him and the television on her way, though she was careful to keep her chin up and her shoulders pushed back. She hoped her posture said something like, *Don't mind my totally naked and inviting body walking directly into your line of sight to get a snack*, or *Please follow me and make me see God on my Kama Sutra tiles.* Either one was acceptable as long as it resulted in an orgasm.

She had been able to register the smallest of movements when she walked by, as if he'd jerked back slightly when shc'd entered the room. Taking that as a win, she continued into the kitchen and headed directly to the set of cabinets that she kept her stash of junk food in. Thankfully, it was directly across the peninsula from the living room, which gave Gavin a pretty clear view of at least her upper body if he turned his head.

Which she hoped he had. *Towel, don't fail me now.* She threw open the cabinet and reached up to riffle through its contents. When the insidious piece of cloth didn't budge, Blake slowly let out all the air in her lungs before taking a deep inhale and reaching even higher.

It did the trick. The towel unfolded from around her and dropped to the floor. "Oh, darn," she said as she turned around and looked at the fabric on the floor as if it had betrayed her, though inside she was doing a jig of joy. But when she sneaked a look at Gavin, he wasn't looking back. In fact, his neck seemed to be so rigidly holding his head facing the TV, his muscles were straining with effort.

This was the second time Gavin had refused to look at her breasts, and it was infuriating. Not even bothering to grab her towel, she walked over to the peninsula and planted her hands atop it. "Oh, come on! It can't be *that* small."

Gavin seemed to startle before his head began doing this weird jerking thing as if part of his brain was telling him to turn his head while the other part stoutly refused to let him do so. Finally, he seemed to settle for slanting his eyes in her direction. "Um, what?"

"Your dick. I mean, you're a fairly big guy. How small could it be?"

He angled his head toward her a little more. "Why are we talking about my dick size?"

"Because it's all I've been able to think about for a week, and you're being really unfair by withholding it from me. And I can't think of any other reason why you won't let me see it besides it being an embarrassment to dicks everywhere."

Gavin looked back at the TV for a moment before shifting on the couch so he faced her more squarely. "I'm so lost right now."

"You're a single guy. I'm a single girl. Seriously, why are we not spending all of our free time naked?"

She watched his lips quirk slightly. "Well, it seems as if you've gotten that party started all on your own."

"You think this is funny? This is so not funny."

At that, Gavin began to laugh. "It's a little funny."

Her shoulders dropped, and she fought back a smile. "I'm dick starved. I haven't been laid in almost a year. How is that amusing?"

Gavin's laughter turned into an air-gasping burst of hysteria. "Did you just say 'dick starved'?" he asked between what sounded almost like sobs.

"Yes," she replied with a stomp of her foot that was totally negated by the fact that she was now also laughing. "I'm so thirsty for it, I feel dehydrated."

That only made him laugh harder, which she hadn't thought was possible. She rested an elbow on the peninsula and plopped her chin into her hand to wait him out. Gavin came back to himself slowly, random chuckles still bursting out of his windpipe like hiccups. Finally, he laid his head back on the couch and let his head flop to the side so that his eyes were on her.

Blake felt her entire body tense up at the seriousness in them. The sudden blast of heat was something she hadn't expected to see after his laughing fit. But as they stared one another down, it became abundantly clear that he didn't find anything funny anymore. And she wasn't the only one who was thirsty.

◆ ◆ ◆ ◆

Gavin wasn't sure which head he should be listening to anymore. Because the one that had turned down the offer of scoping out Blake's chest was starting to sound like a real fucking prude, and it was pissing him off. His dick, on the other hand, seemed to be pointing directly at Blake.

There was a litany of reasons this was a bad idea. Chief among them was the fact that he'd be homeless again if things went south. And odds were very good that things would go south eventually. That was simply how Gavin's life went.

But Blake had already called the landlord about getting him added to the lease, and they had an appointment with him set up for early next week. Surely he couldn't fuck things up *that* fast. Once he was on the lease, she wouldn't be able to toss him out when—whatever was bound to happen happened. Things would be tense, but he wouldn't be homeless. And that thought was enough for him to pat the couch cushion next to him.

Blake tilted her head at him. "With the towel or without?"

"My preference is without, but it's up to you."

She seemed to mull it over for a second, which surprised him. She'd been the aggressor from day one, and it made him wonder if it had all been an act.

"Seriously, it's your call," he said. "I don't want to pressure you into anything."

Blake looked at him like he was an alien. "You're not

pressuring me. I'm just trying to figure out if I'll want the towel for other purposes."

A million things flew through his mind, but trying to figure out exactly what she meant by that was too exhausting to contemplate, so he asked her instead. "What other purposes could it serve?"

Shrugging, Blake leaned forward so that she was bent over the peninsula, her large breasts squashed into the tile. "Blindfold, gag, restraint...lots of things."

Gavin was amazed that someone like this existed, let alone wanted to sleep with him. "That's...probably the hottest thing anyone's said to me in a long time. Maybe ever."

Blake pouted. "Hey. I've said lots of hot shit since we met."

Gavin laughed as he patted the cushion again. "Get your sexy ass over here."

Standing slowly, Blake dragged a finger across the countertop as she walked around it. The act struck him as a bit of a cliché move that still managed to be hot as fuck. Especially when she came fully into the room, and he got an eyeful of her naked body. Smooth, pale skin stretched over a curvy body that was something out of Gavin's fantasies. Her nipples were pink and pebbled on her ample chest. Genetics had been really fucking good to Blake.

She lowered a knee onto the cushion he'd patted, but she didn't sit. Instead, she swung her other leg over Gavin's thighs and settled her round ass on him. Her breasts pushed into his shirt as she rocked into him, her naked pussy rubbing him through his mesh shorts.

He gripped her hips as he encouraged her to keep

undulating into him. His cock was hard—had been since she'd walked past him in the towel—and it demanded more friction. More Blake.

Her breath ghosted over his ear as she panted at the sensation. "I just have one rule," she said on an exhale.

He pressed a kiss to her neck. "Don't worry. I always glove up." Not that he'd had much need to recently. His entire life had been stagnant for months. Maybe even years if he let himself truly dissect it. Until Blake.

Blake chuckled lightly, but it turned into a moan as the tip of his dick dragged across her clit. "I guess I have two rules then."

"What's the other?" he asked as he nibbled on her collarbone.

Spearing her fingers through his hair, Blake yanked just hard enough to pull his head back so he was looking up at her. "This is just sex. Wherever, whenever you want it, I'm down. But I don't do...more. Got it?" Blake was massaging his scalp as she continued rocking into him. There was a slight smile on her lips that took the bite out of her words, but the sincerity was still there. In her eyes, in her tone. And Gavin agreed that it was something they definitely needed to be on the same page about.

"Just so I'm clear, what exactly qualifies as 'more'?" he asked.

Blake stopped moving and looked at him seriously. "Dating, commitment, love. I'm not a puppet, Gavin. No one puts strings on me."

Gavin had to hold in a scoff. He was a disowned college

dropout who could barely make ends meet. He was in no position to offer anyone anything except an orgasm. He moved his hand from her hip and held it out to her. "Deal."

Looking down at his hand, Blake laughed before grasping it. "Good. Now where were we?"

Gavin let his head fall back against the couch. "You were about to make me come in my pants like a teenager."

Grinding down on him harder, Blake let her hands drift down his chest to the hem of his T-shirt, which she promptly yanked over his head. "Was I now? That's pretty sexy, actually."

"Yeah?" he asked.

"Yeah. Knowing I can make you lose it just by rubbing against you. Makes me feel kind of...powerful."

"Well, you haven't made it happen yet. Maybe you're not up for the challenge."

Blake shook her head slightly. "Gavin, Gavin, Gavin. If there's one thing you're going to need to learn about me, it's that I'm *always* up for the challenge." Then her lips were on his, her tongue tangling with his almost instantly.

Gavin raised his hands to cup her face as he sat up straighter. Her gyrations against him sped up, and he let one of his hands drift down her spine until it came into contact with her ass. She was pressed tightly to him, and her tiny frame made it easy for his fingers to keep moving, sliding along her crease and into her wet pussy. He finger-fucked her as she rubbed her clit over the erection in his shorts. He could feel himself leaking precome.

"Oh, fuck, Gavin. Just like that." Blake fucked back on his fingers while still grinding on his cock. The girl should've been a Broadway dancer with the way she could move her body.

"Gonna come for me?" he asked her, more because he felt his balls drawing up tight and less because he was fluent in dirty talk.

But she groaned at his words as if they'd personally traveled down her body and rubbed against her G-spot. "Yeah. So close."

His own orgasm felt like it was zinging down his spine. He sucked one of her nipples into his mouth and pulled on it lightly with his teeth.

Her breathing hitched before her entire body locked up for a brief moment, followed by a bone-deep shudder that thrummed through her entire body.

His release slammed into him a couple seconds later. Jets of come shot all over the inside of his boxers. It would be a total mess, and fuck if he cared. He hadn't even been inside of her, and Gavin had come hard enough to make his dick pulse even after the last of his come had shot out of him.

They panted against one another, still wrapped up in each other. Finally, Blake pulled back. "Having a male roommate was literally the best decision of my entire life."

Gavin laughed as he lightly swatted her ass. "I'm glad."

ELIZABETH HAYLEY

CHAPTER EIGHT

"Have you really not had sex in a year?"

The words startled Blake, who'd been lingering in the euphoria that followed a great orgasm. Once they'd come, they both went to their respective rooms to clean up and change. Or in Blake's case, get dressed. But by some sort of unspoken agreement, they'd come right back out onto the couch and flipped channels until they found a movie they could agree on. It was some comedy that Blake couldn't remember the name of, but it was entertaining enough that she relaxed next to Gavin and let herself get wrapped up in it. Until his words crashed in on her moment. "Yeah. Maybe a little longer actually." She turned her head and smiled at him. "I don't exactly keep a calendar of my sexcapades."

He looked at her thoughtfully before releasing a "Hmm" and then turned back to the TV.

Blake sat up straighter. "You sound surprised."

"I am," Gavin said simply as he continued watching the movie.

"Why?"

Gavin looked at her like she'd lost her mind. It was a look she was actually fairly used to, but she didn't necessarily like it coming from him, though she wasn't entirely sure why. Maybe

67

because he'd seen her naked. "Are you serious? You offered to show me your boobs the first day I moved in. And then you do your"—Gavin flailed his hand toward the kitchen—"towel routine. Not to mention the fact that you've been coming on to me since the day we met."

Blake tilted her head and thought about what he'd said. She could definitely see where he was coming from. Blake did tend to blurt out whatever she was thinking. It just so happened that whenever she was around Gavin, she thought about sex. "Okay, I get where I may have given off a bit of a ho-ish vibe."

Gavin whipped toward her. "Hey, I didn't mean it as an insult. You just seem very...open-minded. It wasn't a diss, I swear."

"Well, I didn't take it as an insult until you started defending yourself."

Gavin opened and closed his mouth a few times before sighing. "I can't tell whether you're fucking with me or not."

Blake turned back to the movie. "I'm not sure either," she said. They sat in silence for a few minutes, and even Blake could tell it was awkward. But she didn't want that between them, so she did what she rarely ever did with anyone. She decided to talk about something personal to her. "I am pretty open-minded, but not in the way you probably meant it. My brain is open in the sense that everything in there comes spilling out at one point or another. So when I'm attracted to someone, I can't process it all internally. It just sort of...seeps out. But the truth is, I'm not attracted to people all that much. I mean, I can objectively *see* that someone is attractive, but I don't *feel* it often. So when it happens, I tend to come on a little strong."

Studying her, Gavin was silent for a beat before he nodded. "Makes sense."

"Really?" she asked dryly. She wasn't told she made sense all that often.

Gavin shrugged. "Sure." His attention drifted back to the TV, but Blake's eyes stayed on him a bit longer. His ability to roll with her quirks was...kind of endearing. Though it also made her wonder if he was even crazier than she was.

Eventually, she became absorbed in the movie again. "This movie is hilarious."

Gavin side-eyed her. "This is a horror movie."

"No way," she said.

"Yes, it is," Gavin said slowly as if that would help it sink in or something. "There have been, like, five gory deaths since we turned it on. And a whole bunch of people died in the very beginning because their plane exploded."

"But they die in such funny ways."

"How is people dying funny?"

"It's not funny when real people die." She gestured at the screen. "Only when these people die."

Gavin laughed. "Why?"

"Take the decapitated guy, for example. The way his head just rolled along the ground afterward, it's funny. And everyone's overacting like it's a spoof or something."

"I don't think the director's intention was for the audience to find someone getting their head sliced off humorous."

"Well, that was his mistake."

Gavin laughed again, louder this time.

"See," Blake said. "You find it funny too."

"No, I find *you* funny." He tapped her leg with his hand. "I'd love to see what you'd actually consider a horror movie."

"I don't think I've ever been scared by a movie," she replied. "The fact that it's not real always keeps me from getting freaked out by anything."

"Oh man, I may have to test that theory. I love scary movies."

Blake shrugged. "Do your worst."

"I will. I'm already running through my mental catalog of horror flicks to scare you with. I bet I can find some that will make you want to run and hide in your closet," he said with a chuckle.

At that moment, Blake was glad Gavin was still staring at the screen. It meant he didn't see the way her entire body tensed, the sweat that seemed to pop up out of nowhere, the shaking of her hands. She didn't want to do this here, with him sitting mere inches away. Jumping up, Blake started toward her room. "This was fun, but I'm exhausted. Night, Gavin." She hated the wobble in her voice, the rigidity of her gait as she walked as slowly as she dared toward her room.

"Oh, um, night," she heard Gavin call after her. He probably thought she was a total whackjob, but she couldn't bring herself to care about that at the moment.

She slammed her bedroom door a little harder than she'd meant to and sagged against it. Closing her eyes, she tried to slow her breathing. The panic felt like it was trying to claw its way out of her skin even though she was desperately trying to beat it back. Her eyes flew open, and she looked to the large window in her bedroom that opened onto the fire escape.

Blake ran over to it, threw it open, and climbed outside.

Rolling up into a tiny ball, Blake rocked back and forth on the fire escape, the movement settling her nerves as fresh, open air flowed around her. The street below her was bustling and well-lit. She wasn't alone. It wasn't dark. She was okay. Everything would be okay.

Blake had no idea how long it took her to calm down enough to come back inside the apartment. She was too exhausted to care about the time or anything else besides making sure all her lights were on. Her entire body felt leaden when she climbed into bed, and she fell asleep almost immediately.

Which was a mistake, because really, after all these years, she should've known what would happen next.

♦ ♦ ♦ ♦

Gavin bolted up in bed, unsure at first of what had woken him. There were a few silent seconds before he heard a noise again. No, not a noise. A scream. He sprang out of bed and ran to Blake's room. He was surprised but thankful that her door was unlocked as he barged through it.

The sight before him paralyzed him for a moment. Blake was writhing around in her bed, muttering words that were unintelligible but in a tone easy to identify. Fear. Gavin forced himself to move, letting one knee rest on the bed as he gripped her shoulders with his hands, firmly but not painfully. "Blake, wake up."

She thrashed against his hold, so he gave her a gentle shake. "Blake. You're having a nightmare. Wake up."

The shake caused her to jolt as if she'd literally just come back into herself. Her eyes flew open, and she scurried up toward the headboard, pulling out of his reach. She stared at him with wild, terrified eyes as she hugged her knees to her chest.

Gavin held out a placating hand. "Hey, it's okay. I was just trying to wake you up. You were having some kind of nightmare."

She looked at him for a few moments longer. She was scaring the ever-loving fuck out of him, and he needed her to talk to him before he started to panic.

"Get out."

Okay, so maybe he should've been more specific when he wished for her to speak to him. Because those words weren't exactly comforting. "Blake—"

"I need you to get out of my room. Right now." Her voice was steady despite the fact that her body was shaking. But it had an eerie calmness that gave him the impression she had a very loose grip on her emotions.

It made the thought of leaving her alone completely unappealing. "I can stay. I don't mind. Do you want to talk ab—"

She leaped out of bed and marched over to the door, holding it open for him in a clear invitation for him to see himself out.

Gavin looked at her for a few seconds before moving. She looked raw in a way that made his chest ache for her, but she seemed to know what she wanted, and that was for him to make tracks out of her room. The only thing he could do was respect her privacy. But before he could leave, he needed to try again. "If you need anything."

"I won't."

Nodding, Gavin walked out of her room, but her voice stopped him before he got more than four feet away.

"Gavin," she said. He turned to face her, and she continued, "I'm not going to want to talk about this tomorrow either."

"Gotcha," he replied before making his way back to his bedroom. He looked at the clock as he climbed into bed. Two a.m. He felt wired, which made it unlikely that he'd fall back asleep—especially when he could hear the *MacGyver* theme playing through the wall—but there wasn't anything else to do but try. His mind wandered as he thought about Blake and all the things he didn't know about her. Logically, he knew that tons of people had nightmares. But Gavin had never seen anyone have one, much less one like that. And he knew that if watching it had been that scary, whatever she'd actually been dreaming about must have been terrifying.

Gavin did eventually doze off again, but it was the type of unfulfilling sleep that made his head feel heavy and his body slow. He had a long day in front of him, and the last thing he needed to deal with was feeling like a zombie, but there wasn't much he could do about it. After taking a quick shower and dressing in a pair of gray slacks and a red polo, Gavin went into the kitchen to find a pot of coffee freshly brewed, but no Blake. He took his time doctoring up his coffee the way he liked it, hoping she'd make an appearance, but she never did. Eventually he had to leave or else he'd be late for work. He spared a look toward her room—and at her closed door—

before grabbing his keys and leaving the apartment. His mind continued to wander to unpleasant things on his drive to work.

When Gavin had told his parents he wanted to major in photography when he was a freshman, they'd laughed off the suggestion and told him to get real and grow up. So he'd gone into prelaw like they'd decided for him—and nearly flunked out of school his first semester. It was then that they'd gotten "real" and agreed to let him change his major. But when he'd brought up photography again, he'd received stern glares and was told he could pick something in business. He'd chosen marketing because it sounded the least brutal, and while his grades had improved, his mood nosedived. He hated everything about school for the first two years. Then something happened between his sophomore and junior years.

Gavin grew a backbone.

Well, a small one anyway. He went into school on the first day and changed his major to photography. He hadn't told his parents about the switch, but what was the worst they could do once the semester was already underway?

He found out the answer to that midway through the semester when his parents had received his interim grades. Instead of calling to yell at him, his father had shown up in his three-piece suit to confront him outside of his residence hall. But Gavin had stood his ground. He wanted to major in photography, and if his parents didn't like it, that was too damn bad.

His father had agreed that it was too damn bad...for Gavin. Because no way in hell was he going to pay for his son to get some "pansy-ass degree" that would leave him "panhandling to earn a living."

So it was there, in front of a crowd of Gavin's peers, that his father had taken Gavin's chance at finishing his education away from him. The semester had been paid, but that was it. Gavin would receive nothing else from his parents until he "came to his senses."

That had been four years ago, and while Gavin still talked to his parents from time to time, their stance hadn't changed. When he was ready to become a productive member of society, they would be there to help him. But they got to decide what "productive" meant, and evidently, Gavin still didn't qualify. So Gavin had been busting his ass to prove that he could make something of himself without their help. But so far, all that had gotten him was work at a portrait studio that specialized in school pictures, which required him to have another job so he could make ends meet.

Gavin parked as close as he could get to the small studio and then hurried inside. They needed to load the equipment and get to a middle school that was about thirty minutes away as quickly as possible. He was mostly quiet through the entire process, including the unloading and setup once they arrived.

"You okay, man?" Anton, a fellow photographer, asked.

"Yeah. Just a long night."

"I hear ya. I was out last night, buying this sexy-as-hell woman drinks, only for her to tell me she doesn't have one-night stands. Can you believe that? I told her she didn't need to stand, and she threw a drink on me. Women." Anton shook his head like he couldn't believe someone had turned him down.

Gavin wasn't sure how anyone ever *didn't* turn him down.

Thankfully, he was saved from replying by a herd of preteens plodding toward him. They all gripped their picture forms as teachers organized them into lines. The first kid to sit in the chair in front of Gavin's camera was a boy in a short-sleeved flannel shirt, and his hair was shellacked down in a way that made Gavin wonder if the kid's parents had sprayed it with a whole can of Aquanet.

"Look up here," Gavin instructed as he held up his finger over his camera. "Smile."

The boy smiled widely, revealing a mouth full of hardware. Gavin definitely didn't miss those days.

The next few kids moved through the process without any fuss. Then a girl walked up, whipped off the shirt she'd been wearing to reveal a neon-pink crop top that said Sexy Bitch, and plopped down on the stool.

Gavin's eyes widened as he glanced around in hopes that a teacher had caught this girl's outfit. If it could even be called that. But no one seemed to notice, which put Gavin in a position that was awkward as fuck. "Uh, are you supposed to be wearing that?"

The girl sneered at him and gave him an attitude that she shouldn't have been old enough to accomplish. "Who are you? The fashion police?"

"No, I'm someone with eyes." The words were out of his mouth before his brain even gave him permission to speak. He blamed it on the sleepless night.

The girl put her hand on her hip. "What's that supposed to mean?"

"It means I'm not taking your picture while you're wearing

that." The last thing Gavin needed was an irate parent or a ticked-off principal calling his studio because he'd snapped a picture of a girl wearing an obscene shirt. No way was he risking his job for this underage rebel without a cause.

The girl scoffed at him. "You're not my dad. You're just some loser who takes pictures. You can't tell me what to do."

He wanted to correct her that he wasn't telling *her* what to do, but was rather saying what *he* wasn't going to do. "Well, this loser isn't taking your picture. Next," he said, a little louder than necessary.

The girl stood and grabbed her other shirt off the floor, pulled it over her head, and sat back down. "Fine. You're lucky I don't want Mrs. Jansen to see my shirt or else I'd be losing it on you."

"Yeah, lucky is exactly what I feel," he said as he snapped a picture of her while she was blinking. Part of him had wanted to refuse to take her picture at all, but he didn't need the headache. This was the best his revenge was going to get.

The rest of the day passed similarly, with the majority of kids sitting pleasantly and getting their pictures taken, while a few punks seemed to need to prove they were badass by giving him a hard time. It was enough to make him jaded with life.

By the time he got home later that afternoon, he just wanted to sit on the couch and unwind. But that plan was cut short when he walked into the kitchen to get a drink and saw Blake sitting on the kitchen counter.

Her eyes lifted to meet his, and she gripped the glass in her hands a bit tighter. "Hey," she said.

"Hey," he replied. Gavin had no idea what to say and no

mental energy to figure it out, so he went to the refrigerator and pulled it open. He grabbed a can of soda and turned to head back out into the living room, but was stopped when she said his name. Letting out a breath, he looked over at her.

"Can we...talk?" she asked.

There wasn't a part of him that wanted to do this now. Truthfully, despite how harsh her dismissal of him had been the previous night, she didn't owe him an explanation. He also had a strong feeling he might not want to know what it was all about anyway. But she was looking at him expectantly, and he found himself unable to refuse her, so he leaned against the counter a little ways from where she sat.

"Sure."

She released a shuddering breath before beginning. "I want to start by saying thank you. I know I was...kind of nasty last night, but my reaction wasn't personal. I don't like anyone to...see me...like that, and I reacted badly. So I apologize, and I appreciate you trying to help me." She took a sip of what Gavin guessed was water before continuing. "That said, please don't ever do it again."

Gavin leaned in, unsure if he'd heard her correctly. "I'm sorry, what?"

Blake looked mildly frustrated at having to explain herself. "Look, I've had nightmares for most of my life. I haven't had one in a long time, but I'm used to them. Well, as much as anyone *can* be used to them. You coming in isn't going to help anything, so I'd like you to not bother."

Setting his drink down, he clasped his hands in front of himself. "I don't know if I can do that."

"What?" Her tone was indignant.

"There's no way I can hear you screaming and not check on you. I'll always be worried someone is killing you or something. I'm sorry, but I can't ignore it."

"I'm not asking you, Gavin. I'm telling you. Leave it alone."

"Not gonna happen."

"God, you're irritating," she said as she leaned toward him. "I have no idea what I see in you."

Her mood seemed to be lifting a little, which surprised him. He hadn't expected his refusal to make her *less* tense, but that was exactly what it seemed to have done.

"What can I say? It's all part of my charm."

She snorted in response, and Gavin knew he could get up and things would be fine between them. But now that she'd brought it up, he was no longer so eager to let it go.

"Wanna tell me what you were dreaming about?"

"No."

The word was immediate and emphatic, so he didn't push it. "Well, I have to say, I'm glad you forgot to lock your door. I was worried I'd have to bust it down." He chuckled softly in an attempt to lighten the atmosphere.

"I didn't forget."

Her reply made the smile slide off his face.

"You didn't?"

She sighed. "No. I never lock my door."

"Can I ask why?"

"It's nothing you need to know about. It won't affect you for as long as you live here."

Gavin sat there silently and examined her face.

As if pressured by his silence, she rolled her eyes and started talking again. "I don't like to feel trapped in small places, okay? So I don't lock my bedroom door, or the bathroom door for that matter, so you may want to knock before going in. And I removed the doors from all the closets in the apartment."

Gavin had wondered about the curtains that enclosed the closets in the hall and his room but figured something had gone wrong with the doors and Blake just hadn't replaced them. "Why?" he asked.

"Tons of people are claustrophobic. This is, like, one of the least weird things about me."

Gavin's voice was soft when he replied. "You looked like you were being tortured last night, Blake. It didn't seem like a typical nightmare to me."

She gave him a challenging look. "An expert on nightmares now, are we?"

He simply shrugged, because the truth was, he didn't know shit about it. But he did know that what he saw the previous night came from a darker place than she was admitting.

Blake pushed her glass away and slipped off the counter. "Either way, it's not a story for today. I have some...quirks. But you won't ever have to explain yourself to me. I'm only asking for the same courtesy."

The curious part of Gavin wanted to push, but the rational part knew it wouldn't get him anywhere. It wasn't the jovial Blake he'd come to know standing in front of him. No, the person in front of him presented as more of an emotional Fort Knox. If she didn't want to confide in him, he knew she wouldn't, and nothing he said would change that. "You got it."

"Good. Thanks," she said before leaving the kitchen and heading for her room.

Trying to ease the tension between them, he called her name and got her attention before she disappeared down the hallway. "About you not locking the bathroom... If I hear the shower running and assume you're naked, do I still have to knock?" He smirked at her and was happy to see her return it.

"Only if you're an idiot," she replied with a saucy grin before continuing on her way.

Gavin remained at the table for a few minutes, thinking about his confusing yet adorable roommate.

MISADVENTURES WITH MY ROOMMATE

CHAPTER NINE

"Come on. Let's go," Blake said.

Gavin looked over from the counter to where Blake had come out of her room. She put on her second earring—some sort of silver and gold combination of dangly pieces that sparkled in the light. She was wearing a loose royal-blue button-up shirt with sleeves that came just over her shoulder. As she got closer, he noticed that the material was sheer enough to see her bra underneath, which he supposed was intentional. For some reason, nothing about Blake struck him as accidental.

He let his eyes drift down her body as he took in how tight her skirt was, and how high her shiny black heels were. Somehow the straps that wrapped around her ankles made her legs appear longer. At the sight of her, the chewing of his Corn Pops slowed almost to a complete stop, but finally he was able to get them down. "You look... Jesus," he said, letting the spoon he was holding drop into the bowl before swiveling the bar stool so he could face her completely. "You look amazing. Where are you going?"

"We."

"Sorry. Where are *we* going?" he asked, realizing quickly that he was more than happy to follow her wherever it was she was headed.

"A retirement party. I can't go to this thing *alone*. I barely know anyone."

Gavin wondered why that was a problem for Blake. She didn't strike him as the type of person who'd let appearing solo at an event faze her. He was hoping she'd asked simply because she'd enjoy his company, but he didn't want to ask.

"Why are you telling me about this now?"

Blake shrugged. "I decided a few minutes ago that I wanted to invite you."

Gavin chuckled at her bluntness, even though at this point it didn't surprise him. "I'm flattered. How do you know I'm even free for the night?"

"You're eating cereal for dinner on a Saturday, and you're already in that old pair of mesh shorts that I doubt you'd ever wear in public."

Gavin looked down at his basketball shorts from his senior year in high school. Only small pieces of the navy-blue vinyl lettering remained, and the silver mesh had thinned considerably over the years. "Fine," he said, rolling his eyes in feigned annoyance. "When do we have to leave?"

"Ten minutes."

Gavin widened his eyes. "What! That's not even enough time to take a shower."

"Sure it is. Most of my showers are less than six minutes. And that's with shaving. I bet you can be in and out in four."

Gavin let out a sigh that ended in light laughter. "Okay. I'll do my best. It might be more like fifteen minutes though."

Her dark-red lips turned up into a broad smile. "Thank you."

"You're welcome," he muttered in a tone that sounded way more disappointed than he actually was.

"I'll wait in my room. Guy and Baby are arguing about who has to be on top when they have sex later."

"Sounds...interesting," Gavin said, though he wasn't sure that was the right word for what it was.

"It always is with them."

Twelve minutes later, he came out of the bathroom in a light-pink dress shirt and dark-gray slacks. He was rolling up his second sleeve when Blake's voice caused him to look up from his arm.

"Damn, you clean up nice." She had a tip of her finger to her lips, and he could practically feel her gaze creeping slowly down his body.

His hair was still damp from his shower, but once it dried, the loose curls would thankfully find their place without needing any real taming to make his hair look like he'd put some effort into it.

"How are Guy and Baby?"

"Guy's on top."

Gavin laughed before asking, "This outfit okay?" He smoothed the front of his shirt to make sure there weren't any more wrinkles in it. He'd brought it into the bathroom with him, hoping the steam would take the place of ironing, which he would've done if he'd had more than two minutes left to get ready.

"That outfit's *more* than okay," she answered. She gestured at his body as she spoke. "The way your pants sit perfectly at your hips, slim through the leg until they hit the top of your shoe. If I didn't know better, I'd say you have a strong sense of fashion, Gavin Gibson."

Gavin laughed as he walked into the kitchen and grabbed his wallet off the counter. "Thanks. Now tell me about this party," he said before opening the door and holding it for her.

In the cab on the way to the party—which was being held at a local high-end restaurant that had been rented out for the event—Blake had filled him in on the essentials. An attorney named David was retiring after twenty-five years in the field. Gavin wasn't sure how Blake knew the guy, but he figured if she wanted him to know, she would tell him.

"Who should I say I am?" Gavin asked on their walk from the cab to the restaurant.

"I wouldn't worry about it," Blake said. "I doubt anyone will even ask."

Gavin nodded, hoping that was the truth because he certainly didn't want to say he was Blake's boyfriend, but saying he was a friend also seemed strange because why would someone bring a friend to a retirement party? "So...you can just bring a guest to this?"

"Sure. Other people are," she assured him.

Gavin took that as a sufficient answer because...well, it was the only one she'd provided. He nodded again and opened the door for Blake to enter.

The Italian steakhouse was larger than Gavin had expected and seated at least forty people comfortably among six tables dressed with pristine white linens, which Gavin knew he'd get sauce on within minutes of his entrée coming out. Which reminded him... "Do you know what the dinner choices are? This place looks like it'll be pretty good," he said, scanning the culinary options around him—a table with an assortment of cheeses, arancini, bruschetta, and several other appetizers that Gavin couldn't recognize from a distance.

"No idea what they're serving. My guess is Italian food," she said, a slight smirk on her lips.

"You think you're pretty witty, don't you?" Gavin teased.

Her smile broadened at his comment. "Possibly."

"So who is this guy who's retiring?" Gavin asked as he made himself a plate.

"What do you mean? He's just a guy."

"I don't know. I guess it struck me as strange that you'd go to a retirement party for someone unless you were close to him. I've had like...a million jobs, and I've yet to go to one of these," he said.

"Well, glad I get to see you lose your retirement party virginity then," Blake said.

Laughing, Gavin looked around at everyone, his neck craning around a woman who was standing nearby. "So which one of these gentlemen will I be giving it up to tonight?" he asked.

Blake stared at him but said nothing.

"I took it a little too far, didn't I?"

"A little," she said.

Blake looked around at the tables. Most of the people were already seated, but some were up mingling or taking pictures. She nodded in the direction of three men who were laughing by the bar, but he wasn't sure which one was the guest of honor.

Though it really didn't matter. He didn't plan to start up a conversation with any of these people, though he'd obviously engage in one if someone spoke to him. He wouldn't consider himself antisocial, but the crowd of professionals—most of whom appeared to have way more money than he had—reminded him more of his parents' acquaintances than anyone he'd hang around with. Or Blake for that matter. Which only made him wonder what exactly the connection was between Blake and this lawyer.

"So how do you know this guy?" Gavin asked, unable to tame his curiosity any longer. He followed Blake toward two seats near the end of one of the long tables, and they settled themselves in.

"Oh, um..." She dipped a piece of bread into some oil and popped it into her mouth, swallowing completely before answering. "Sorry, this bread is amazing," she said. "I worked for him for a little while."

"Oh yeah? Doing what?" Gavin was surprised. Working for a lawyer would had to have paid more than her current jobs. Not to mention that it probably required a certain level of education or training that Blake hadn't mentioned when they'd had their discussion about school. And her presence at this party suggested she'd left on good terms. It didn't add up.

"Nothing exciting. Filing things, answering phones, that sort of stuff."

"Let me guess," Gavin joked. "You left when you got an opportunity that you couldn't pass up, and that's how you found yourself working with me at The Coffee Bean."

"You know it," she said. "The Bean's my dream."

Gavin laughed before taking a drink of the wine that had been set in the middle of the tables for everyone to share. "I think it's closer to your nightmare."

The second the words left his mouth, he saw Blake tense, but it was too late to take them back. It was exceptionally poor timing considering what he'd learned about her only a few days ago.

"I'm sorry," he said softly. "I wasn't...I wasn't thinking." As if by instinct, his hand went to her arm to comfort her, and surprisingly she didn't pull away.

"It's okay," she said. "This night isn't about that. Let's try to have a good time."

Gavin sighed audibly in relief. The last thing he wanted to do was ruin *this* night too. "Okay," he said, wanting to get back to a more lighthearted conversation. "So you left a gig at a law firm to make caffeinated drinks for stay-at-home moms and overworked professionals. Sounds like a solid choice," Gavin joked.

"Would you be surprised if I told you how low that decision ranks on the list of ones I wish I could take back?"

"Nope," Gavin said with a laugh.

"Besides, the Bean's gotten better the last few weeks actually. Helps when you have someone there you like and can joke around with."

Her comment seemed sincere, so he wasn't sure why he had to ruin the little moment they seemed to be having by saying, "Yeah, I know. I like Maddie a lot too."

Though she shook her head, his joke seemed to amuse her. "You know, you're pretty witty yourself," she said.

"Why, thank you." He pushed his bread plate to the side so he could make room for the salads the servers were setting down.

Though Gavin would never have ordered a salad with goat cheese, walnuts, and strawberries in it, he had to admit it was damn good. He finished the last few bites and then leaned back in his chair, highlighting the fact that he'd eaten his salad at a rate that was more suited for a ravenous bear than a human. He cleared his throat awkwardly as his eyes darted to the people around him who were slowly putting forkfuls of salad into their mouths. And despite Gavin's initial reluctance to speak, he felt the need to say something since he wasn't eating anymore. And that something involved asking all the people around him how they knew David. Apparently, that was the only question he could think of tonight.

"He's one of the partners at the firm," the man across from Gavin said. "There are five of us in total, and we've all known him for over fifteen years," he said, gesturing to the surrounding men and women. "Except for Veronica, who's only been with us for...what? Seven years, is it?"

Veronica shook her head but laughed. "I've been there twelve, Mark. You always do this."

Mark laughed, making his large belly jiggle against the table. He reminded Gavin of a red-haired Santa Claus. "Well, it feels like we met just yesterday," he said. "What about you two? How do you know Dave?"

"Oh, I don't," Gavin said. "My...Blake used to work for him. Right?" He looked to Blake to expand on the conversation he'd somehow started, but she had her mouth full, so her answer was limited to a nod.

"Is that right? How long ago?" Mark asked. "I can't seem to place you. Though as you just saw, my memory leaves something to be desired."

Blake's eyes shot to the ceiling as if she were trying to remember when she'd worked there. "A while ago," she finally said. "Maybe six or seven years ago."

"Huh," Mark said with a shrug. "Sorry. We get so many interns and temps through that place it's hard to keep track of everyone who comes and goes."

"I'm sure," Blake said. "No worries. I barely remember anyone who worked there either."

"Except Dave, I guess," Veronica added.

"Right, yeah," Blake said. "Most of the stuff I did was related to his cases."

"Oh, okay," Veronica said. "Did you film your part of the video yet?"

"Video?"

"Yeah. His wife's making a video for him, and she wants everyone to say a few words to Dave in lieu of gifts."

Until Veronica had mentioned gifts, Gavin hadn't even noticed that Blake hadn't even brought a card with her.

"Oh. Okay, yeah, I'll find her later and make sure I record something," Blake assured her. "What did all of you say? I'm never any good at these things."

Veronica spoke first, explaining that she talked about how much it meant that Dave made her a partner and that she was going to miss his homemade donuts on the first Monday of each month.

Mark said he congratulated him and told him that if he played golf without him, he'd be sorry. Though it was mainly because Mark was so horrible that David would be missing out on a chance to feel good about his own game—which Mark said was almost as bad as his.

Each person on their end of the table had a story about Dave or something to thank him for. Gavin wondered what Blake would say, but he was sure she wouldn't want him watching while she filmed.

"What about you?" a young colleague named Samantha asked. "What are you going to say to Mr. Belson?"

"I think I'll..." she started. "I'm sorry, what did you say?"

"I asked you what you're going to say on your part of the tape."

"David *Belson's* tape?" Blake said, her eyes noticeably widening.

Samantha looked confused, and Gavin could understand why. It didn't make sense that Blake seemed surprised that the video would be for the guy retiring.

"Speak of the devil," Veronica said, nodding to the door where a man had just come in.

The applause and cheers that followed his entrance made it obvious to Gavin that the man was David Belson. He was also *not* one of the men that Blake had pointed to earlier when Gavin had asked who the party was for. But before he could ponder the question any further, he noticed Blake's porcelain skin somehow get a little whiter, as if the man's presence had caused a physical reaction in her that she hadn't been expecting. He couldn't even begin to guess what the hell was going on.

She watched him make his way around the room toward their table as he said his hellos. Slowly, Blake set down her fork and pushed her chair away from the table. Then she turned to Gavin. "I'm gonna grab a drink from the bar. Do you want anything?"

Gavin looked at his glass of wine, which was still half full. "No thanks. I'm good."

"Can I get anyone else anything?" she asked politely.

They all muttered that they were okay and no thank you, which was good because Blake didn't seem like she was even focused on their answers.

And as Gavin watched Blake walk toward the bar, he realized there was something he wanted after all—to know how the hell Blake knew David Belson.

CHAPTER TEN

Blake took her shot of tequila from the bartender and asked for another before he'd even turned away. What were the chances that David *Belson* was the lawyer who was retiring? She hadn't seen him in ten years. And that felt like a lifetime ago. She'd been a different person then—one who needed help from others instead of relying only on herself.

And David had been the one to help her. She hadn't given him much thought since. And now here he was, somewhere in this room, probably no more than fifteen feet away. It wasn't that she didn't want to see him so much as she didn't want to see him with Gavin there. Speaking to David would undoubtedly stir up emotions she'd rather not feel at all, let alone right now.

When her friend Emily had suggested this party as one that Blake and Celeste should go to, all she'd told them was that it was a retirement party for a lawyer named David. Emily hadn't told her his last name, and that wasn't odd. In fact, she rarely ever gave her more than a few quick facts about the events. And up until now, it hadn't been a problem.

Over the past seven months or so since Emily had gotten the job at the steakhouse, Celeste and Blake had attended parties here for people they didn't know at all. Somehow they were usually able to fly under the radar, get some free food, and make it out undetected. But that wouldn't be the case tonight. When Blake had realized that the lawyer this party was for was David Belson, she'd run through any and all options that might allow her to escape this cosmic disaster unscathed, but she couldn't come up with anything. And a part of her felt that their presence here together was more than a freaky coincidence.

She took the second shot that the bartender had set down in front of her before her thoughts went back to Gavin. She felt bad that she'd left him with the partners at the law firm, but... Okay, that was a lie. She didn't feel bad exactly so much as she felt conflicted. Her choices were to stay and talk to them herself or let Gavin chat with them. And since he'd been the one to begin the conversation, she didn't feel as guilty as she probably should have at leaving him with a group of people he didn't know.

Plus, knowing Gavin, he was probably holding his own over there. Unlike her, he seemed to *enjoy* talking to people. He was sociable. He was friendly. He was open. He was warm. Come to think of it, he was all the things Blake wasn't. Which might explain why she enjoyed his company. He compensated for traits Blake lacked; he was the yang to her yin.

The thought made her turn toward him. But as soon as she spun around, she caught a glimpse of the only face she should recognize besides Gavin's.

David.

A few more wrinkles had settled in around his eyes, and his gray hair looked considerably whiter. But his smile held the same warmth it'd held ten years ago, and the sight made the memories of that time flood through her.

She was so caught up in staring, she'd forgotten that David might recognize her as well.

Until his eyes caught hers for a brief moment.

At first it was a flash—a quick glance in her direction before he returned his gaze to the man sitting across from him. But in an instant they were back on her, as if it had taken him a few moments to process the sight before him. The person he'd been speaking to was still talking, but she had a feeling David had stopped listening. He put a finger up to the man and said something before pushing his chair out and standing.

Though he'd obviously recognized her, and there was no escaping whatever conversation was coming, she turned toward the bar again, not wanting to watch him approach—as if facing the opposite direction would allow her some emotional distance she knew she wouldn't get. She was aware of her shaking leg and the way she spun the cardboard coaster—a clear sign of her nervousness that she didn't do anything to stop.

"Ms. Monroe?" David asked, putting a gentle arm on her back before probably realizing the contact might be too much for her and letting it drop. "Is that you?"

Blake took a deep breath and stood taller, squaring her shoulders before turning toward him. "In the flesh," she answered with a quick smile that didn't show her teeth.

David shook his head quickly like he'd just seen a ghost and was trying to decide if the image was real. "How are you? God, I've thought about you so many times since the hearing."

"I'm good," she assured him, and she meant it. Though she was far from what most people would consider normal, she wasn't the mess David probably remembered.

"That's so good to hear," he said. And he gave her one of those smiles that seemed more out of relief than of genuine happiness. "Tell me what you've been up to. What's it been? Ten, fifteen years?"

"Just over ten," she answered. "And don't be jealous, but I have two jobs and barely any money, so not much has changed for me in the employment department."

David chuckled, but it faded quickly. "As long as you're getting by and you're healthy, that's all that matters."

Blake nodded in agreement, and the two were quiet for a moment until David spoke again. This time he seemed a little more hesitant. "What about a significant other? Boyfriend? Girlfriend? Do you have anyone you're—"

"You know I don't get attached."

"I do. But I thought maybe ten years might have changed that," he said, though she recognized the disappointment on his face.

"I'm hoping to bang my roommate soon if it makes you feel any better." She pointed to where Gavin was seated. "He's the hot blond talking to some of the people from your firm."

David let out a loud laugh and shook his head in amusement. "I see you haven't grown a filter in the last decade."

This time Blake was the one laughing. "Some things never change, I guess."

"Guess not," David said. And then, "I should probably get back over to my table, but I have to ask... What are you doing here?"

Blake bit her lip if for no other reason than to hold back

the smile she could feel trying to escape. She raised an eyebrow before asking, "Do you really want to know the answer to that?"

He seemed to think over her question for a moment before saying, "You know what? Knowing you, I don't think I do." Then he put a hand on her shoulder and rubbed it gently, cautiously. "It was good seeing you, Blake. If you ever need anything, give me a call, okay? I mean it."

She nodded, but for some reason, she found it difficult to speak.

"And I hope you and the hot blond have a good time tonight. Enjoy yourselves."

She watched him walk back to his table, her shoulders falling with relief that she hadn't had to think much about her past and that David had been so accepting of her presence here. Taking a few deep breaths, she prepared herself to go back to the table and act like the universe hadn't just fucked with her.

But as soon as she turned toward Gavin's table, he was inches away from her face, a brow furrowed in what Blake identified as curiosity. "Whatcha doin'?" he asked. "You've been gone longer than I thought you'd be."

"Miss me already?" She tried to keep her voice light, but she was sure her expression betrayed her. She couldn't let Gavin find out how she knew David. She'd already had enough judgment for a lifetime.

"Yes," he said. "But more importantly I thought maybe you missed your old colleagues. I'm surprised you don't want to catch up with them more. It's been a while since you've seen them."

"Yeah, it has. So long actually that they barely remember

me. Guess I don't make as memorable an impression as I thought." She held up two fingers to the bartender so he'd bring more shots. She'd offer one to Gavin, but if he didn't want to drink it... Well, she'd never been one to let top-shelf liquor go to waste. David did say to have a good time.

Gavin studied her for a moment, not even responding when she offered him the shot the bartender had just set down. "Blake," he said, "I know this probably isn't any of my business, but you asked me to come here, so I kind of *feel* like it's my business now." He sighed, and Blake could sense the uncertainty in it—like he was unsure about whether continuing was a good idea, but he knew he had to. "Did you ever work for Belson's firm?"

She hadn't been sure what he was going to say, but his question didn't surprise her. "Not exactly," she admitted. It was more like Belson had done work for *her*. Though she hadn't had the money to pay him, David had offered to help her for free after her caseworker—who'd been an old friend of David's—had reached out to his firm.

Gavin set the shot back down and crossed his arms over his chest, looking more guarded than she'd ever seen him. But one thing he didn't look was surprised. "Okay," he said, drawing out the word. "So then I gotta ask," he said. "How do you know David Belson?"

"I don't," she answered immediately, hoping her quick response would solidify its truth for him.

His head pulled back in confusion. "What do you mean you don't know him?"

"What do you mean what do I mean? I don't know him,"

she repeated. "Exactly what I said. I've never even seen the guy before tonight."

Gavin shook his head and rubbed his hands over his face. "Really? So you just like...came to some random guy's party?"

"Yup."

"I don't get it. What exactly are we doing here if you don't know this guy?"

Blake smiled as she picked up the shots and handed one to Gavin. "Eating and drinking for free," she said. "My friend Emily works here, and she tells me when private parties over thirty people are coming in. That's enough that if anyone here wonders who we are, they'll probably just assume we know someone else." This would've been the truth if she hadn't happened to know the person retiring. "Usually Celeste comes with me, but she got stuck working, so you were her stand-in tonight."

"Oh." Gavin had been listening to her speak but hadn't responded, and his blank expression revealed nothing about what he was thinking. He opened his mouth a few times but closed it each time without saying anything. Finally he seemed to find the words. "So you crash retirement parties?"

"Basically. Yes," she answered. "Or birthday parties, engagement parties, weddings, and baby showers. If she isn't working, Emily tells whoever is to set two extra places. They always have extra food at these things, so why waste it?" she asked, not expecting an answer. "We even did a rehearsal dinner one time. That one was a mistake in hindsight. Someone asked me to give a speech...and the bride's father hit on Celeste... It was a mess."

"Huh. Well, I guess crashing parties is a better scenario than what I thought was going on."

"What did you think was going on?" Blake wasn't sure she wanted to know, but her curiosity got the better of her.

"I don't know. Like...anything, I guess." He pointed back to the table where the other partners were still seated and enjoying the entrées that had been brought out. "When you left, they said they were defense attorneys, and I thought maybe—"

"That I needed defending?" Blake raised an eyebrow in amusement.

The gesture seemed to relax Gavin, who took a deep breath and let his arms fall to his sides. "I don't know. I mean I didn't think you murdered anyone or anything."

"Neither did the jury."

Despite her serious delivery, Gavin barked out a laugh. "Stop," he said. "My thought was totally valid. You brought me to this guy's retirement party, and you said you worked with him. Then no one remembered you, but you talked to him for like five minutes, so I just thought—"

"That I killed someone," Blake said, interrupting Gavin's rambling. Though she had to admit she found it cute.

"No! I definitely didn't think you killed anyone. Aggravated assault at most," he joked, making Blake smile. "I honestly didn't really think about what the crime might've been. I just thought maybe you needed legal representation for something and David Belson got you off."

Blake tried to suppress her smile at his words. "I'm fairly confident when I say that David Belson could never get me off."

"That's not a visual I want to think about," he said, making the two of them burst out laughing. When they finally calmed down, Gavin's expression sobered a bit, and he leaned against the bar.

"So, wait, why was Belson talking to you then if you don't know him?"

"He saw someone he didn't recognize and came to see who I was and what I was doing here."

"Oh shit. Really?"

"Yeah. But don't worry. I used my charming personality to convince him that we should be allowed to stay. He told us to have a good time, so we're totally good." It was as close to the truth as she could provide at the moment.

Blake had been focused on her explanation, but when her eyes went back to Gavin's, they seemed to twinkle with something she couldn't quite identify. "What?" she asked, suddenly nervous about what Gavin's reaction was going to be.

He shook his head. "Just you," he said with a laugh that alleviated the tension she hadn't even realized she'd been holding. "You're something else, that's all."

She didn't know what that "something else" was, but she had to agree.

CHAPTER ELEVEN

As the night went on, Gavin loosened up and even found himself having fun at a party that he wasn't technically invited to around people he wouldn't otherwise have ever associated with. Not that he did much interacting with anyone other than Blake. Once they returned to their table and had eaten one of the best meals Gavin could remember eating in years, they'd had a few more drinks and dessert before heading home.

By the time they got back to the apartment, they could barely make it up the steps without stumbling into one another. Or maybe that was only true for Gavin. Blake seemed more accustomed to the effects of the alcohol than he did. It had been a while since Gavin had been drunk, and the fuzziness inside his head as he carefully ascended the stairs felt unfamiliar. He leaned against the wall outside the apartment as Blake unlocked the door and pushed it open. Then he gestured for her to enter because he wasn't going to let her open the door for him *and* walk through it before her.

"Crashing retirement parties is fun," he said, collapsing onto the couch. "Oooh, we should try a family reunion next. Really test our skills," he suggested as he thought about how they'd somehow been able to carry on a conversation with strangers.

Blake laughed, but it seemed half-hearted. "I don't think I'm ready for that yet," she said, taking a seat next to him.

Gavin looked at her—studied the way she rubbed her fingers over her thighs like she didn't know what to do with her hands. He also noticed the way her eyes were focused on the coffee table in front of them. He wasn't sure if she was just a little out of it from the alcohol or the long night, but he could swear that she was avoiding eye contact with him. "You okay?" he asked.

This time she looked at him. "Yeah, fine, why?" she said casually, though when he saw her eyes, he could tell she looked anything but fine. There was a blankness to them. Like she was thinking about something far away.

He shrugged, unsure of whether to press the issue. But she'd opened up the door by asking him why he thought that, so he decided he might as well answer. "You seem...distant or something all of a sudden. Did I say something? Or *do* something?"

"It's stupid," she said.

"It's not stupid if it upset you. Tell me so at least I'll know not to do it again." It reminded him of when he'd seen Blake having the nightmare, and he wondered if the two were somehow connected.

Blake was silent, and Gavin did his best not to fill it. If she were going to share whatever this was with him, she'd have to be the one to decide to do it. Finally, she sighed. But he wasn't sure what that meant exactly until she spoke a minute or so later. "The family reunion thing," she began. "It's probably the one type of party I have no experience with. I could probably fake my way through a bris easier than I could a reunion. At least those have an actual focus. I mean, I know the focus is on cutting off a part of someone's penis, but still," she said with an awkward laugh.

Gavin remained quiet but took note of the fact that she'd made a joke during what seemed like should be a serious conversation. "Can I ask why you hate family reunions?" It wasn't that Gavin couldn't relate to the dread that accompanied those types of get-togethers, but he had his own reasons for disliking them. He guessed Blake did as well.

"It's not that I hate them so much as it is I've never been to one."

"Never?" Gavin couldn't hide his surprise.

She shook her head. "My family wasn't the reunion *type*, I guess."

His eyes locked on hers, and he couldn't identify what he saw in them. There weren't actual tears behind them—at least none that he could make out. But there was a heaviness to them, a weight that let him know Blake had more layers to her than he could probably ever peel back. But he had to try anyway. "What type *were* they?"

Blake's head was spinning, and it wasn't from the alcohol. She could handle way more than the six shots she'd had over the course of three hours. But what she couldn't handle was how easy it felt to share things with Gavin that she typically kept to herself. When he'd mentioned the family reunion, it had struck a nerve for her, but she couldn't explain exactly why. She'd accepted her family situation—or lack of one—when she was a kid. It wasn't like coming to terms with her troubled childhood was anything new. Still, sitting here with Gavin, feeling close to someone for the first time in as long as she could remember, did things to her that she'd rather not think about.

"They were..." She struggled to find a way to describe her parents that was truthful, yet didn't reveal every last detail about them. "They weren't around a lot," she finally settled on. She deliberately omitted that the reason was because they were neglectful deadbeats who'd rather think about where their next fix was coming from than whether their daughter had eaten that day. "I'm not close with them."

Gavin nodded like he understood, but she knew he didn't. And in his defense, she hadn't given him the opportunity to try. "I'm not too close to mine either," he said.

"Oh yeah? Why?" She suddenly found herself hoping that Gavin's parents were pieces of shit, too, so she could commiserate with him, but even she knew that was a horrible wish to make. She also knew that they'd wanted him to go to college, so the chance of them being complete lowlifes was slim.

"We don't agree on...well, anything, now that I think about it." He laughed, but Blake heard sadness in it. "What about you?"

"Same," she said, because there was no way she could get into all of her shit right now. Or maybe ever. Her story was raw and messed up and so fucking crazy that it caused a type of pain most people hadn't ever felt. At times, she thought she should've been embarrassed by her past. But she wasn't.

She never had been. Shame hadn't ever been a factor in her decision to keep her history to herself. The opposite had been true actually. She felt a kind of pride that she'd been able to overcome such a troubling upbringing, and had somehow come out of the mess relatively free from any real damage.

Sure, she was guarded and cautious and private. But those were bandages more than they were scars—mechanisms put in place to protect her from any further pain and hopefully allow her to heal. At least that was what Shrink One, Two, and Three had told her. Even as a child, her life was like a Dr. Seuss book of psychiatric professionals. "My parents didn't really have the time for me, let alone the time to get to know me," she added, because not only was it the truth, she also found herself wanting Gavin to understand her a little better. And for the first time, she welcomed that connection with someone.

The realization was frightening.

She'd been looking down at the floor as she'd spoken, but something brought her eyes up to Gavin's. "Well, that's their loss," he said as he cupped her cheek. "Because you're worth knowing."

Blake's lips parted at his words, but it wasn't to speak. The way he stared at her—like he wanted her, wanted the *real* her, had Blake feeling vulnerable. And though the emotion was a familiar one, it wasn't how she remembered it. It wasn't threatening or uncomfortable or complicated.

And as Gavin's mouth pressed against hers, she found herself wanting to open up to him in more ways than one. Immediately, her body relaxed into his as he traced his fingertips over the delicate skin of her shoulder and down her arm. It was a sensation that would normally have gone unnoticed, but for some reason, she reacted to his every touch in a way that felt more than physical.

Suddenly her whole body was on fire, alive in a way that had her gasping for air like she'd forgotten how to breathe. Gavin's mouth was everywhere—nibbling down her collarbone and over her chest as he slipped her shirt over her head in one fluid movement that almost didn't register in her brain.

Her breaths were choppy, needy as he kissed his way down her stomach, which flexed with urgency. But she didn't want this to feel rushed. She wanted this time to be slow and gradual, a steady climb toward a release she desperately needed. Her skin tingled at his touch as he dragged her pants down at a torturous pace. He looked amused watching her squirm, her body silently begging him for more. Then, hooking one finger under the elastic of her thong enough to graze the area that wanted him most, he rubbed gently. She could feel how wet she was, how slick and ready she must have felt on his fingertip before he finally pressed inside her enough to somehow dull the ache she felt without actually satisfying it.

He took his time there, stroking her walls with a shallow touch that had her fantasizing about getting on top of him and riding his fucking hand until she came all over it. When he removed his finger from her, the emptiness she felt was almost unbearable, but thankfully he'd only paused to remove her panties. "Too much," she said when Gavin's mouth found her clit and sucked hungrily on it. His movements slowed, but they were no less pleasurable, and she had to practically push his head away to keep herself from losing it.

He gave her a few kisses to the inside of her thighs before bringing himself back up so he could look at her. "I love making you feel like that, getting you so close you can barely stop yourself," he said. "Let me make you come."

His words weren't as much of a plea as they were a command, and Blake knew better than to resist. As much as she liked the way Gavin teased her with his tongue and fingers, she wanted to feel his cock inside her. She was ready to combust just thinking about how good it would feel to have every subtle ridge and vein massaging deep within her, and she wasn't sure how much longer she could wait before she came from Gavin rubbing over her.

She thought about how wet the outside of his pants must be from the contact with her slick pussy, and she wondered if he was as ready as she was, barely able to hang on as he ground against her. "Need you inside me," she huffed out, causing a low groan to escape Gavin's lips.

"Say that again," he said.

"I need you, Gavin. God...so bad...I'm gonna..." She wasn't able to utter the last word before Gavin climbed off her, pulled his pants down, and reached for his wallet to withdraw a condom.

Gavin finished undressing—first his shirt, one button at a time, and then the rest of his clothing until he was hovering over her, all of him exposed to her. He reached up to grab his cock and slid the condom over it as he held his position above her.

"Gavin, I don't think I've ever come without physical contact, but watching you do that may change that," she said.

"That sounds like a challenge."

He was so hard, and the tip of him was nearly purple as he stroked himself. She wanted that inside her now. "It's not. Come here," she said, gripping his ass and pulling him down onto her.

At first, the contact with his skin was enough, but before long she was begging for him to enter her. Thankfully, this time he complied, pressing into her gently, slowly, until he thrust so deep inside that she almost came from the force of it. Her breath hitched as he drove into her again and again, the head of his cock stroking her slick walls so rhythmically that she could hear how wet she was for him. It wouldn't be long before she was pulsing around him, her body shuddering in ecstasy.

She dug her fingernails into Gavin's back as she struggled to hold off, but it was a futile effort. A few more drives of his hips and she'd plummet into a place that would have her lost in sensation. Gavin moaned one of those low moans that had her feeling the vibration from his chest in hers, and when he told her to let go, she exploded around him, her walls clenching his shaft so tightly that she was sure he could feel everything inside her too.

She watched him intently as he sought his own release: his face straining with pleasure, his abs flexing as he thrust into her.

She listened to his heated groans as his body shook and he emptied into the condom. He seemed to spasm for an intensely long time, the ecstasy etched on his face. When he was finally done, his eyes opened, and they caught hers for a moment before he closed them again, this time more relaxed.

"Jesus, I feel..." he said. "I don't know what I feel."

And neither did she.

CHAPTER TWELVE

"If you could be any animal, which would you be?" Blake asked as she leaned against the counter at The Coffee Bean.

Her question had come out of nowhere, and it took Gavin a minute to process it as he scrubbed down the counter with a rag. "Which would I *want* to be, or which would suit me best?"

Though she rolled her eyes at him, the grin on her face belied any real exasperation. "Why do you always make everything so complicated?"

It was a good question. Gavin's life had always seemed more complicated than it should've been, but he didn't think she'd want to hear about all that—and he wasn't sure he wanted to share it with her—so he said, "Because I like annoying you. And I genuinely don't know which you meant."

"Which fits you best," she clarified.

Pursing his lips, Gavin thought about it for a few seconds before he resumed his scrubbing, mostly just so he'd have something to do with his hands. "I have no idea," he said finally.

Stomping her foot in clear agitation, Blake glared at him. "I'm bored, and you're not making it any better."

"And identifying my spirit animal would make you less bored how exactly?"

"It won't. But it'll help prevent me from picturing you

naked."

Gavin turned his head so he could look at her. "Why would I want to help prevent that? Our best moments have involved us being naked," he replied with a small smile he hoped came across like the sexy smirk he intended it to be. Ever since the retirement party the previous week, Gavin and Blake had spent the majority of their free time naked together.

"Because if I picture it, I'll want it to happen, and since it's my lifelong dream to serve heaps of caffeine to ungrateful corporate robots, I refuse to do anything that could get me fired from this fine establishment." She wagged a finger at him. "I will not allow you to lead me astray, young man."

"Gotcha," he replied. "Can I lead you astray at home later?"

"Depends."

"On?" he asked with a raised eyebrow.

She leaned toward him, pushing her boobs together to make her cleavage pop out of her shirt. Since it was almost closing, the place was empty, and Gavin was grateful for it. For reasons he didn't let himself examine, he didn't want anyone else catching a glimpse of Blake's chest.

The scent of her fruity body wash filled his nostrils as she closed in on him. Her fingers grazed his shirt as they drifted from his bicep to his chest and back again. Giving him a sultry look, she whispered, "What animal, Gavin?"

"Oh, for fuck's sake," he said, which caused her to step back as she laughed. "I honestly don't know. Which one would *you* be?"

"A koala," she said without hesitation.

Gavin pondered that for a second before asking, "Why a koala?"

"They're small and cute and look cuddly, but if they don't want you in their space, they'll claw your face off."

"That's...violent."

"Sometimes ya gotta show a bitch who's boss," Blake explained.

Gavin chuckled. "You've had to show a lotta bitches who's in charge, huh?" he asked as he turned to straighten the coffee cups. Expecting her to laugh, Gavin turned toward her when he didn't hear a sound.

She was looking at him, but she definitely wasn't laughing. "What if I said yes? Would you think less of me?"

Her question made a thought pop into his mind, and his brain latched onto it until he couldn't help but ask about it, even though it wouldn't tell her what she wanted to know. "Does it matter what I think?" The question came out with a sincerity he wholeheartedly meant.

She was quiet so long, he wasn't sure she was going to answer. When she finally spoke, it was nearly a whisper. "Yeah. It does."

He turned to face her fully and slumped back against the counter. This question was clearly something she wanted a serious answer to, and Gavin wanted to make sure she knew he was being straight with her. "No. It wouldn't make me think less of you."

"Really? You seemed kind of scandalized when you thought Belson helped me beat a murder rap."

A rumble of a laugh tumbled out of him. "I wasn't

scandalized. I was just making sure I didn't have to start locking my door at night."

Her eyes stayed on him, the serious expression not moving from her face. "I'm not violent though. You know that, right? There have been times in my life I've had to do...things. Things I'm not super proud of, but that were necessary at the time."

It seemed really important to her that Gavin understood this about her, though he had no idea why. Especially since it had never occurred to him that Blake was a violent person. A little out there, sure. But not aggressive or harmful. "I know. I never thought you were."

She studied him for a second before saying "Okay" and turning away to start going through the closing-down procedures.

Gavin stared after her, confounded by, well, pretty much *everything* about his roommate. She was mercurial and zany and intense and complicated. But she was also oddly solid and intelligent and fun and simple. Blake was an enigma, and Gavin found himself wanting to figure her out more than he cared to admit.

◆ ◆ ◆ ◆

Blake needed to get a handle on herself. She'd spilled more to Gavin since he'd moved in than she had to anyone else since she'd been a kid and learned the hard way that the things that made you tick were best kept secret from others. Even Celeste didn't know much about her. Not really. And Blake liked it that way.

Whenever people had heard about what her life had been

like growing up, they looked at her differently—started trying to put her behavior into some kind of context. But Blake liked to think of herself as beyond comprehension. There was no putting the pieces of her childhood together to make a clear picture of who she was as an adult. She looked nothing like the box she'd originally been packaged in.

So she let people see only who she was *now*. And they could decide to take her or leave her from there. Most people decided to take a pass on knowing her, and that was completely fine. Blake wasn't able to handle a lot of different people in her life. But she knew without a doubt that she wanted to handle Gavin. He'd slid into a comfortable nook in her life, and she wanted to keep him there. Which was why what he thought of her had been so damn important. She'd chased away tons of roommates, but she wanted to hang onto Gavin's friendship for as long as she could.

"Ready to go?" Gavin asked from behind her. She turned to look at him, and he continued. "Patrick said we could head out."

Patrick was the assistant manager who closed most nights. He was pretty chill and sometimes let them leave a few minutes early as long as the place was prepped for the next morning. "Yup."

They called goodbye to Patrick before walking out and heading for Gavin's car. They were quiet, but it was comfortable between them. At least to Blake, who typically never found herself very at peace in silence. Once they arrived at the car, Gavin unlocked her door and held it open for her, closing it behind her after she climbed in. He settled into the driver's seat seconds later and began driving them home.

"You working at the bar tomorrow night?" he asked.

"Yup. Saturday too." She usually worked Monday and Friday nights, and Sunday afternoons, but she offered to fill in for another bartender Saturday as well. She usually liked having at least one weekend night free so she could pretend she had a social life, but money was money. She'd been hoping to get more weeknight hours, but the small bar usually didn't get busy enough during the week to need more than one bartender, and those nights were usually worked by the owner. He'd offered to let her work as a server if she needed more hours, but that put her too much in the fray. She liked having a bar—or counter in the case of The Coffee Bean—between her and the masses.

"Maybe I'll come see you."

"Yeah?" she asked, knowing that he'd heard the delight in her voice at the prospect.

"Sure. Maybe I'll be able to drag Simon out with me."

"That'd be cool. I can let Celeste know, and he can call her a pizza again." She smiled widely as Gavin laughed.

"Yeah, he's a great guy, but he's got no game at all."

"And you do?" she asked, quirking an eyebrow.

"Well, since I had you offering to let me round second base within hours of me moving in, I'd say I've got plenty of game."

"I never said you could touch them. I just felt bad for you and wanted to throw you a pity flash."

"If you say so."

Blake's mind wandered as they drove. Something was

bothering her, and even though she told herself she shouldn't bring it up, that was exactly what she did as Gavin parallel parked in a spot near their apartment. "Are you banging other girls?"

His hand on the steering wheel slipped a little, causing the car to straighten out too early, so Gavin had to pull out and attempt to park again. When he'd nestled them safely into the spot, he cut the engine and looked over at her. "Does it change anything between us if I am?"

Blake thought for a second. "No. As long as you're not using me to cheat on some poor girl who thinks you're the future daddy of her children." That answer wasn't *entirely* true, but it was close enough. Blake didn't particularly love the idea of sharing Gavin because she was selfish as hell, but she knew she had no claim to him. If he was out laying pipe every other night, that was his business. She'd just be extra vigilant to make sure she stayed stocked up on condoms.

"Okay. Good," Gavin said before he threw open his door and got out of the car, leaving Blake sitting there dumbfounded. He stood on the curb and looked at her through the windshield, probably wondering why she was still sitting in his car, so she hurried out and fell into step beside him.

They made it halfway down the block before she threw her hands up. "Jesus Christ, are you going to answer my question or not?"

"I thought I did."

"Gavin, I swear to God, I don't want to have to shank you out here and leave you for dead."

She saw his shoulders shaking in her periphery and knew

he was laughing. The asshole. "I thought you said you weren't violent," he said through his laughter.

"I'll make an exception for you."

Out of nowhere, he slung an arm around her and pulled her close as they walked. "What's the matter? Don't wanna share all this hotness with anyone else?"

"Well, now I wish I could *give* you to someone else."

"That's not true," he taunted.

"Did you take ecstasy at some point between work and here? And if so, why didn't you share?"

Laughing again, Gavin pulled her even closer. "Now you know damn well I always share," he said suggestively.

"Yeah? With how many women?"

Gavin pulled back a little so he could look into her eyes. She wasn't sure what he was looking for as he studied her, but his smile morphed into something smaller and sweeter. "None. I have my hands full with you."

His answer caused a burst of warmth to rush through her, though she did her best to hide it. "Not yet you don't. But as soon as I get you in that apartment, your hands will definitely be full of me." They shared a smile, but the moment felt incomplete somehow. So Blake said the only thing she could think of. "My hands are full with you too."

And from the way Gavin squeezed her shoulder, she assumed he was happy to hear it.

CHAPTER THIRTEEN

Gavin felt like his skin could barely contain the want coursing through him. It was almost how he felt when he was behind the lens of a camera, out in the world, exploring the beauty that was so easy to take for granted when you didn't stop and look for it. And as he spun on Blake when she closed the door to their apartment and crowded her with his body, he was so fucking glad he'd stopped to look closer. That he hadn't dismissed her as some goofball he worked with. Because even though he hadn't known her long, he did know there was so much *more* to Blake. And despite the fact that she'd probably never want to tell him any of it, he was drawn to it nonetheless.

"You drive me crazy, you know that?" he whispered against the skin of her neck as he nuzzled into her.

She laughed huskily. "It's a short drive with me."

His lips curled into a smirk as he kissed along her jaw. When he pulled back, his eyes locked with hers, and he found himself unable to look away for a minute. After a beat, her eyes slid closed, and he put his lips on hers in a kiss full of passion. He cupped her cheek, tilting her head so he could have better access. Then he let his tongue push into her mouth, her moan vibrating through him as if it had a direct line to his cock.

She wrapped her leg around his thigh as if she was trying

to climb him, so he took the hint and hoisted her up. "Need... naked...now." Her words came out in harsh pants.

"Your place or mine?" he asked her. His hands were kneading her ass as he sucked and nipped along her throat.

"I...I want...Christ," she gasped and speared her hands into his hair and pulled. When he was looking at her, she continued, "I can't think with you doing that."

"Sorry," Gavin said, though he knew his tone told her he was anything but.

She gazed at him for a second, her lips pursed like she was mulling something over.

"Do you want to stop?" he asked, her hesitation making him unsure.

The appalled look on her face was enough indication that that was not something she wanted. But the "What are you, insane?" she yelled at him also helped chase his doubts away.

"Then why are you doing that weird thing with your mouth?"

She smirked. "Oh, baby. I can do *tons* of weird things with my mouth. If you're nice, I'll show you sometime."

His dick, which had flagged a bit, really liked that answer.

"I don't want to have sex in either of our rooms," she said.

"Okay." Gavin waited for her to continue.

She released a deep breath before speaking again. "If you think it's too weird, we don't have to. It's just something I've always wanted to do, and I thought...maybe...you'd be up for..."

"Spit it out, Blake."

"Remember later that you told me to spit."

"I'm seriously going to drop you on your ass if you don't

tell me what you want."

"You're so salty," she said as she tightened her grip on his neck. "Let me whisper it to you." She leaned in, nipping at his earlobe before saying, "I want you to fuck me on my Kama Sutra tiles."

And his cock was fully back with the program. "Yes. Let's do that," he replied quickly as he began carrying her toward the bar top that separated the living room from the kitchen. He dropped her onto it and then urged her to lie back so he could climb on top. He rocked against her as he kissed her deeply.

Clothes began flying every which way as they ripped them off one another. But before Gavin completely shucked his pants, he reached into them and withdrew a condom from his wallet.

"Like a fucking Boy Scout," Blake said.

"With you around, I'm not taking any chances of being unprepared." Gavin ducked his head for a second before refocusing on her.

"Just so you know, I've been tested since the last guy I messed around with and have an IUD. If the same goes for you, maybe we could..."

She didn't finish her sentence, but Gavin couldn't help but tease her. "I don't have an IUD."

She rolled her eyes at him. "Forget I said anything."

He dipped down and kissed her before drawing back and looking her in the eyes. "I've been tested since my last partner too."

"So you wanna?" she asked.

Caressing her skin at her hairline with his thumb, Gavin

said, "Say what you want, Blake."

She huffed. "You're so annoying. Fine, do you want to fuck me bare? Because I could really—"

Her sentence was cut off by Gavin's lips on hers because he couldn't keep them off her.

Gavin grinned against her mouth. "You trust me that much?"

"I trust you maybe a little too much," she whispered.

"I think you trust me just the right amount," he said before dipping his head so he could lick and suck on her nipples, which caused her back to arch off the counter.

"Need you in me," she whimpered.

Gavin guided himself into her with one long, smooth motion. He thrust into her as his fingers toyed with her nipples, and she writhed beneath him like she was trying to simultaneously get away from him and also pull him deeper inside her.

Gavin looked at the tile beneath her, and the dueling erotic sights caused his balls to draw up. He wasn't going to last, and he needed her to catch up with him. His hand drifted down her body until it reached her clit. As soon as he made contact with it, she bucked harshly.

"Fuck, yes. Right there."

He continued to play with her clit as he drove into her, his hips pumping wildly as his orgasm rested on a precipice. Two more thrusts and he was hurtling over it, his release slamming through him and emptying into her. Her slick walls felt amazing around his sensitive cock, but he didn't let himself bask in the afterglow.

Scooting back, he licked a trail down her stomach before he arrived at his destination and began lapping at her clit.

She thrust her hands into his hair, holding him in place even though he had no intention of going anywhere. He pushed into her with two fingers as his tongue continued to flick at her sensitive bud.

He darted his eyes up to see the ecstasy on her face. He watched as her shoulders lifted off the tile and her entire body shook with her orgasm. He felt her wetness envelop his fingers. It had his spent cock twitching, but he ignored it to climb back up her body and press soft kisses everywhere he could reach.

Her chest rose and fell quickly as she tried to catch her breath. He planted his elbows on either side of her head and looked down at her. He knew the smile on his face looked smug, but he didn't give a shit.

"Proud of yourself?" she asked with a smile of her own.

Gavin shrugged his reply, but his smile grew wider.

"Well, you sure as hell should be. I bet these tiles learned a thing or two tonight."

Gavin buried his face in her neck and laughed like he couldn't remember ever doing after sex before. It was cathartic in a way he never would've expected. Though he guessed being with Blake in any capacity was likely to have that effect on him. Not that he'd ever tell her that.

CHAPTER FOURTEEN

Blake had been busy since she'd walked into Reed's. There had evidently been some kind of softball championship for grown men earlier in the day, and they'd all decided Reed's was the perfect place to end their failed attempt at recapturing their youths. Blake was never more thankful to have a bar between her and the crowd since she only came up to mid-gut on most of the softball players. And the more pitchers of beer they had, the more they leered at her.

She really hoped she didn't have to junk-punch anyone before the night was over.

As she filled an order of Bud Light pitchers and shots of tequila, her eyes snagged on Gavin, who was sliding onto a stool at the bar with Simon. She held up a finger to them and carried the drinks over to the cocktail waitress to deliver.

"It's packed in here," Gavin said when she reached them.

"It's been like this all night. I'm about to pull the fire alarm to clear some of them out."

Gavin laughed. "That'd only clear some of them?"

"Yeah, the regulars know better than to give up their seats unless they hear sirens." Even though Gavin was laughing, Blake wasn't kidding. Joe Reed, the owner of the bar, had actually installed a fake fire alarm that didn't alert first responders in case a fight broke out or some other emergency. Blake was sure it was illegal as hell, but it served its purpose. "What can I get you guys?"

"What do you have on tap?" Simon asked.

Blake ran through the five beers and then recited the twelve more they offered in bottles. Both guys ordered lagers in a bottle, which was easy enough for Blake.

"Can you start us a tab?" Gavin asked.

"I could if I didn't plan on collecting payment in sexual favors later," Blake replied.

Simon nearly choked on his beer as he attempted to prevent himself from spitting it everywhere.

Shit, Blake thought. Maybe Gavin didn't want Simon to know they were having sex. "Sorry. I was just...kidding?" she said as she looked at Gavin for some guidance on how to handle her big mouth.

Gavin smiled and took a sip of his beer before saying, "If you were kidding, I'm going to be disappointed."

A huge wave of relief swept through her at his words. While she would've understood if Gavin had wanted to keep their arrangement private, it made her feel good that he didn't mind if his friend knew.

"But really," Gavin said, his smile gone. "Start us a tab. We don't want you to get into trouble."

The reality was, Joe was cool with his bartenders giving out some free drinks to their friends as long as they didn't abuse the privilege and the friends didn't order top-shelf shit. But she didn't want to argue with him, so if Gavin wanted a tab, she'd start him one.

Simon's eyes ping-ponged between them as if he was trying to figure them out. Since it wasn't Blake's place to fill him in on any more than she already accidentally had, she excused herself to tend to some other patrons.

She was restocking the beer cooler when she heard someone say, "Jesus Christ, what does a thirsty broad gotta do to get a drink around here?"

"Walk into the men's room and get on her knees," Blake replied without looking up at the voice she knew so well.

Celeste chuckled. "The crew in here tonight looks like they couldn't find their dicks with an extra hand and a map."

"Guess you'll have to help them then," Blake said as she made room for the last bottle, and looked up at Celeste and Emily. "Can I get you anything, Em?"

Celeste squawked. "What about me?"

"I know what you want, lush." Celeste rarely ordered anything other than a margarita when she went out unless she was celebrating or depressed.

"I'll have a cosmo," Emily said.

"'Kay. I'll deliver them over there." She pointed to where Gavin and Simon were sitting.

"Ooh, you didn't tell me Simon the Pizza Man was going to be here," Celeste drawled.

"Who?" Emily asked.

"Ya had to be there," Blake said to Emily. "And I said Gavin was bringing a friend," she added to Celeste.

"But you didn't tell me it was hot Simon. Hmm..." Celeste tapped her lips with her finger. "I wonder if he'll let me scream a different name in bed."

"I feel like you're skipping a lot of steps," Blake said, eyeing Celeste as Celeste eyed Simon.

"What steps?" Celeste asked absently.

"Like him remembering who you are."

Celeste waved her off. "Such unimportant details."

Emily and Blake shared a look before amused smiles spread across their faces. It was hard not to be entertained by Celeste.

"Go say hi while I make your drinks," Blake said. She watched the two women approach Gavin and Simon and then set about mixing their cocktails. When she plopped them down on the bar in front of her friends, she said, "Has everyone met Emily?" She gestured toward her red-haired friend as she spoke.

"We have now. I was just thanking her for inviting us to crash that party," Gavin said with a smirk.

Sexy bastard.

Celeste's affronted face tore her attention from Gavin. "You went to the party without me?"

"Yeah. You couldn't go."

"That means you can't go either."

Blake eyed her friend. "That's clearly not what it means since I went."

"You're a terrible friend," Celeste said as she pouted.

"Speaking of bad friends," Simon cut in, "I watched that *Teen Mom* show you were talking about. Why does Simon want to be friends with Farrah so much? She's an awful human being."

Celeste blinked at him for a few seconds before putting

her elbow on the table and resting her chin on her hand. "I think you're my soul mate."

Simon looked stunned for a second before a shy smile crept over his face that he tried to hide by taking a sip of his beer.

"Blake!"

She turned at the sound of her name being yelled to see the other bartender Steve holding his hands up with an exasperated look on his face. "I need to get back to work before Steve goes postal. I'll stop back in a bit."

Returning to work kept her busy, but it didn't stop her from sneaking glances over at her friends repeatedly throughout the night. They looked like they were having a great time, and it made her a little jealous that she couldn't be having fun with them. Celeste seemed to be hanging on Simon's every word—an action that seemed to be mutual. And Emily and Gavin were gabbing with a few people sitting near them. Finally, around midnight, the crowd thinned out a little, and she got to spend a little more time talking to them.

Her friends had just taken another round of shots when Celeste stood up. "Okay, this girl's had enough. Simon, your place or mine?"

Celeste's words made Blake remember a time she'd uttered the same phrase to Gavin. The memory turned her on a little.

Simon looked gobsmacked as his head shot around to look at all of them before returning his gaze to Celeste. "Um, I have a roommate."

"Heavy sleeper?"

Nodding, Simon responded, "Total stoner."

"Your place it is then. One of my roommates stays up late drawing chalk pentagrams on our floors."

Celeste dropped two twenties on the bar and then grabbed Simon's hand to pull him toward the door. It caused Simon to frantically pull cash out of his wallet before stuttering out quick goodbyes to the rest of them.

"This is too much," Blake called after them.

"It's for getting me laid," Celeste called back, making a bunch of the customers turn to stare at them.

"She's...forceful," Gavin said with a laugh.

"You have no idea," Blake replied. She looked at Gavin, and their eyes caught, holding one another's stare as if in a trance.

"I think that's my cue to leave too. I have to work brunch tomorrow." Emily rolled her eyes as she spoke.

"Want me to call you a cab?" Blake offered.

"To drive me two blocks?" Emily countered.

"You're not walking by yourself," Blake said, her tone serious and unbending.

"I'll walk her," Gavin said as he drained his beer. "Then I'll come back and keep you company until you can leave."

Blake looked at her watch. "That's still an hour and a half from now," she warned him.

He shrugged. "I got nothing else to do."

Emily asked how much was still owed on their tab, and Blake replied, "You know I only ever charge you girls twenty each. Celeste took care of your portion."

Fishing a bill out of her purse, Emily handed it over. "Nah, that was her payment to her pimp." Emily laughed at Blake's groan.

"Can I settle up when I get back?" Gavin asked.

"When we get home, you mean?"

Gavin looked at her with impatience she was pretty sure was an act.

"Stop being difficult. I can hold your tab for you," Blake said instead of teasing Gavin further. She'd only rung up every other drink, so the thirty dollars Simon had absently thrown down covered it anyway, but part of her knew that having a tab open guaranteed Gavin would come back. Not that she doubted his word, but she'd learned early on in life that it was always good to have a little insurance.

Emily gave her a small wave as Gavin shot her a quick smile. She stood there and watched them walk out, wondering how she'd managed to snag such a decent guy as her roommate. She was sure fate would eventually intervene and fuck it all up for her, because that was how her life went. But for now, Blake was going to enjoy having a good man sharing her apartment, who also fucked like a stallion.

She turned back to the other customers, silently acknowledging that this was probably the happiest she'd been in her entire life. And that fact simultaneously thrilled and scared the fuck out of her.

◆ ◆ ◆ ◆

Gavin walked slowly back to the bar, enjoying the crispness of the evening. He and Emily had exchanged some small talk on the way to her apartment—a walk that took less than ten minutes—and she thanked Gavin profusely for accompanying her. Not a single part of Gavin had minded walking with her. It prevented him from sitting at the bar by himself for quite as long while he waited for Blake to finish up.

He knew he didn't have to wait for her. Blake managed to get herself home every night she worked. But there was something appealing about walking home to their apartment together. Maybe he could turn it into some kind of extended foreplay. The thought made his dick pulse with arousal.

When he arrived back at Reed's, he noticed the crowd had lessened even more since he'd been gone.

"Hey. I saved your seat," Blake said when she saw him.

Gavin slid onto the barstool and looked at the glass of water Blake had set there, presumably to save his spot. "Thanks."

"The walk go okay?"

"Other than the mugging and gang war we got caught in, yeah, it was fine."

Blake shook her head. "Such a smartass. You want another beer?"

"Nah, I'll drink the water."

"Okay. I need to start cleaning up so we can get out of here."

Gavin nodded before looking around. "Where'd the other bartender go?"

"He was first off. Since it slowed down, Joe sent him home. Joe's in his office if we need him."

"Gotcha."

"You really don't have to stay if you don't want to."

"I want to."

Blake smiled at him. He couldn't help the feeling that they were shamelessly flirting, even though neither had said anything remotely provocative. *Score one for foreplay*.

He watched her move effortlessly around the bar, wiping things down, straightening bottles, washing glasses, and all the other things that went into shutting the place down. There were still a few stragglers at the bar—regulars, Gavin would guess by the way the staff joked around with them. There was also a fairly large group by the pool tables that kept ordering drinks from the cocktail waitress, who Blake had introduced as Dana.

"These assholes keep ordering one drink at a time," Gavin overheard Dana say to Blake.

"Okay, take them this one, and then I'll call it."

Dana nodded and took the Captain and Coke to the group. Once it was delivered, Blake yelled, "Last call, everybody."

"We still got half an hour," one of the guys yelled.

"Yup, half an hour to nurse one more drink," Blake called back as she continued to do what she needed behind the bar.

"That's bullshit. We're not ready to go home yet."

"Didn't say you had to go home. Plenty of after-hours places in the city," Blake returned, still keeping her attention away from the pool table.

"Forget her, Al. We'll leave when we're good and ready to go," one of the others said.

Gavin gripped his glass a little tighter. These guys were pissing him the fuck off.

"Where's that waitress? I want another drink," rang out

from the direction of the pool table.

Gavin saw Dana deflate and start in their direction, but Blake waved her off. "I got it."

His eyes widened as he watched Blake round the bar and make her way over to the guys. She had to pass him on the way, and Gavin reached out and tugged on her wrist. "You want me to go over with you?"

A slow smirk overtook her face. "Not unless you want to piss them off."

"Well, no, I don't want that. Not that I care if they're pissed off, but I don't want—"

"Gavin," Blake interrupted.

"Yeah?"

"I got this. But you're cute when you're worried."

Gavin scoffed. "I'm cute all the time."

"Very true. I'll be right back."

Trying to watch Blake out of his periphery without appearing like he was staring at the group of dickheads was a little difficult, but Gavin managed.

The sound of balls clacking together, followed by one rolling down a pocket, filled the room. "What do we have here? A pool shark?" Blake asked.

"Yeah, he wishes," someone joked.

"Don't we all. Then I wouldn't have to have a group of guys trying to make my life difficult," Blake responded.

"Aw, darling, we're not trying to do that. We're just having a good time."

"Well, good. I'm glad you guys had a nice night. Why don't you tell me what else you want to drink, and then I'll have Dana close out your check?"

"You trying to get rid of us?" one of the guys said with a teasing lilt in his voice.

"Yes," Blake replied, which made all the guys laugh.

"Okay, sweetie, we'll close out."

"Thanks, guys."

Blake returned to the bar and picked right back up with what she'd been doing. Quite a few scenarios had played out in Gavin's mind for how he thought that interaction was going to go, and all of them ended with the police being called. He couldn't believe the guys had backed down as soon as Blake had gone over. Though the more he thought about it, the more he understood.

Blake had an air about her. A confident you're-not-going-to-get-one-over-on-me-so-don't-bother-trying air. She was somehow charismatic and intimidating. Those guys had probably been drawn to her while all the same being unwilling to tick her off.

It wasn't more than ten minutes later that the group abandoned the pool table and headed for the exit. One guy, a fairly tall guy in a dark green Henley, detoured over to the bar and leaned his forearms on it.

Blake looked over at him. "You need something?"

"Yeah, I was hoping to get your phone number. Maybe take you out sometime?"

Blake smiled, but Gavin was happy to note that it didn't reach her eyes. "Sorry, but I'm already someone's sugar mama."

Gavin's eyebrows shot up in surprise. Only Blake would say some shit like that.

Green Henley guy laughed. "Guess it's my loss then."

"Guess so."

The guy knocked on the bar with his fist once before making his way to the door.

"All right, you two. That's your cue to leave," Blake said to the remaining guys at the bar.

"What about him?" one of them asked as he tilted his head in Gavin's direction.

"He's my bodyguard for the evening," Blake replied. When neither man made any attempt to move, she sighed loudly. "He's my roommate. He stuck around to walk me home. Now go away so I can lock up."

Both men quickly rose and grabbed their jackets from the backs of their chairs. "You know we gotta watch out for our favorite bartender."

"Yeah, yeah, you just say that to get free drinks," she teased.

"You know it," one said with a laugh before they both waved goodbye and left. Blake followed them and locked the door behind them.

"That's Ned and Carl," she explained when she came back. "They always wait with me until all the customers are gone. Not sure what they think they're going to do if something happens. I'm pretty sure my boobs weigh more than either of them."

Gavin laughed. "That's nice of them though."

"Yeah, it is," Blake said softly. She emptied her tip bucket, counted it quickly, and yelled for Joe.

The older man popped out of the back a minute later.

"How much?" he asked with his hand outstretched.

"One fifty," Blake said as she handed her tips over.

Joe went and opened up the register. "Everything okay tonight?"

"Yup."

"Good." Joe put the smaller bills in the register, and then pulled out a stack of bills and counted some off. When he was done, he closed the register and handed the money to Blake. "Be safe."

"Always," she said with a smile. She slipped the bills into her purse before looking at Gavin. "Ready?" she asked.

"Whenever you are."

"Let's go then. Have a good night, Joe."

"You too," he replied before he went back behind the bar.

Gavin followed Blake out into the night. It seemed a lot darker than when Gavin had returned after dropping Emily off. He looked up and saw that it was cloudier than it had been earlier. "Oh shit," he said as he stopped dead in his tracks.

"What?" Blake asked.

"I forgot to settle up my tab."

Blake grabbed his sleeve and yanked. "Simon left more than enough. Don't worry about it."

"I need to tip you at least."

"Oh, you're going to give me a tip all right."

A laugh burst out of Gavin. "You're such a pervert."

"Totally," she said with a small laugh of her own.

At that moment, Gavin felt a large drop of water hit his head. "Don't even tell me," he muttered. Seconds later, the skies opened up, and Blake and Gavin found themselves caught in a downpour. "Should we try to get a cab?" Gavin asked over the torrent.

"Are you crazy? We're only three blocks away. Let's make a run for it." Blake grabbed his hand and threaded their fingers together as they began to run down the sidewalk.

Gavin easily kept pace with her shorter stride, though his breath was still choppy due to the simple fact that neither of them could stop laughing. They reached their building breathless, drenched, and smiling.

Blake unlocked the outer door and threw it open so they could dive inside. Their laughter filled the quiet hallway as they dripped puddles on the floor. Gavin ran his hands through his hair, squeezing the excess moisture from it. He looked over at Blake, who was wringing out her shirt. Their gazes locked, and the laughter slowly died down. It was replaced by a searing heat despite the fact they were both freezing. Before he even had time to think about it, Gavin was on her, pushing her back against the wall and devouring her mouth.

When he trailed kisses down her neck, she gasped, "You do the hottest shit." She gripped his hair and forced his head up so they could kiss again.

Gavin lowered his hands to her ass and hoisted her up, which prompted her to wrap her legs around his waist. He ground his hard cock into her as she gyrated against him.

"Upstairs," she panted. "Gonna...get...arrested."

Gavin gave her one more deep kiss before dropping her legs and giving her a swat on the ass. "After you."

"The *hottest* shit," she muttered as she started up the steps.

Gavin followed close behind, but was careful not to touch her. When he got his hands on her again, there was no way he'd be able to take them off until they were both breathless on whatever surface she wanted him to fuck her on.

Opening the door tested Gavin's patience since Blake dropped the keys twice before finally unlocking it. Gavin kicked it closed behind him as his hands reached for Blake. Their lips fused together as they ripped wet clothes from one another's bodies and let them *thwap* onto the floor. Tracking water through the apartment wasn't a concern at the moment.

"My room," Blake said, and that was all the direction Gavin needed. He backed her that way as he divested her of any remaining clothing and began groping and kneading her flesh in a way that demonstrated his rabid desire.

She plopped back on the bed and he quickly lowered himself on top of her. There was no waiting, no buildup. Gavin needed to be inside of her like he needed his next breath. He settled between her thighs and pushed into her in one long, smooth thrust that left her moaning beneath him.

"Harder. Fuck, please, harder," she begged.

Gavin sat back on his heels and lifted her legs, pressing them toward her chest before he set a rougher rhythm, pushing and withdrawing from her quickly and fluidly.

Her one hand reached for her pillow, and she grasped it tightly as she groaned in pleasure. The other caressed her breast and tweaked her nipple. There was nothing sexier than Blake touching herself while she rocked with his thrusts. The sight was almost too much. "I'm close," he warned.

"Me too," she whispered.

He pumped his hips even faster, hoping to get her to crest the peak before he did. Seconds later, she was yelling out her orgasm, her nails raking down his abdomen. He rode her through it before his pace stuttered, and he pushed into her as deeply as he could as his own release shot out of him.

He rocked into her gently until his cock was milked dry. Slowly slipping out of her, he let his body fall forward, though he was careful to brace himself on his elbows to keep from crushing her.

After a few moments, Blake smiled up at him. "That was quite a tip," she teased.

"I've never gotten any complaints," he replied before he lazily kissed a laughing Blake.

CHAPTER FIFTEEN

"Shit. These things are never gonna dry," Gavin called from the fire escape in Blake's room. Their clothes had been outside since last night, and they were still pretty damp.

"What?" Blake yelled from the shower.

Gavin walked toward the bathroom, peeking his head through the doorway. He had to admit he liked that Blake had taken to leaving the door open when she showered lately. She'd told him that she couldn't stand the way the small room steamed up when the door was closed, but he liked to think it had more to do with the fact that whenever Gavin walked by, he'd catch a glimpse of her reflection in the mirror, all wet and warm and...

Suddenly, Gavin remembered he was supposed to be talking about something, but watching Blake rub body wash over her breasts and stomach had caused all thoughts of anything else to vanish. However, seeing Blake's clothes on the bathroom floor made his memory come back to him. "I said our clothes are never gonna dry out there."

"How's that possible? They've been out there for over a day."

"It was a little chilly last night."

"Oh yeah. That's true."

"Plus, it's still overcast. My jeans are pretty wet. And the white shirt you had on looks like it's getting rust stains on it."

She let out a frustrated curse. "That's my last Reed's shirt that I haven't ruined. Can you grab everything and throw it in a trash bag? I was gonna go to the laundromat anyway today. Give me whatever you need washed, and I'll do it while you're at work."

"That'd be awesome!" Gavin said. "You sure you don't mind? If it's too much for you to take—"

"You're acting like I'm offering to be a surrogate for your firstborn. I'm doing laundry."

The comparison she'd chosen to make was a strange one, but the point had been made all the same. She was a friend offering to throw a few things in the wash for him. "Okay, thanks. I'll leave the bag in your room. I gotta get going. I'm cursing whichever manager decided to put me in charge of the daycare pictures today. Tabitha and Jamie are doing high school sports teams."

"Ugh, daycare pictures sound brutal. You should do more than curse them."

Gavin laughed. "When I need help thinking of my revenge, I'll be sure to consult you."

"You better," she said, followed by, "Have fun."

"I won't," he promised her. "You're naked and wet, and now I have to leave. I hate this job even more now, and I didn't think that was possible."

"Goodbye, Gavin," she said. And somehow that made him smile.

◆ ◆ ◆ ◆

"Morning, Linda," Blake said after pulling open the door to the laundromat and slinging the gigantic trash bag full of clothes over her shoulder.

Linda looked up from whatever trashy magazine she'd been reading behind the counter. "Well, if it isn't the emo Mrs. Claus," she said in the same monotone voice she used every time she spoke about anything. "I'd ask where your elves are, but I'm guessing even *they* find you intolerable."

Blake bit the inside of her lip to hold back a laugh, and only when she was safely facing the washers—and away from Linda—did she let herself smile. "You're a trip, Linda. You know that?" She plopped the bag onto the metal table and began pulling clothes out of it. But she stopped midreach and looked over at Linda again. "Oh my God. I can't believe I didn't think of it until now," she said.

"I have no interest in knowing what you're thinking of, but I know you'll tell me anyway, so go ahead."

Blake could barely contain her excitement. "Linda Tripp. That's your new name."

"Marvelous," she replied with her signature indifference.

"Ha!" Blake laughed. "I didn't even see it until now, but the physical resemblance is uncanny." She approached the counter where Linda was sitting on her wooden stool. "Straw-like hair, shoulder pads, a face that looks like a cross between John Goodman and Marilyn Manson."

"You done?"

"Almost. Have you ever wiretapped a phone?"

Linda stared at her, and the silence only amused Blake more. "I'm impressed you even know who she is. I've got feces in my large intestine older than you."

"Well, that's...gross as fuck." Blake hardly ever met people who were as odd and disturbed as she was, but she'd met her match in Linda. Which was one of the reasons she went to this laundromat over the one that was two blocks closer to her apartment. The strange Asian man who asked for her help with his crosswords wasn't nearly as entertaining as the gem sitting in front of her.

Blake returned to the washers and began tossing in some of the clothing. There were definitely at least two loads, and it crossed her mind to separate the clothing so that Gavin's was in one washer and hers was in another. But she ultimately decided that if she could mix bodily fluids with the man, she could certainly mix laundry.

"Whose boxers are those?" Linda called from her stool. She'd turned her head toward Blake, but her body was still facing the front of the store. She reminded Blake of an owl without the wisdom.

"Your mom's," Blake said. The ridiculousness of her comment only made it funnier to her, but she managed not to laugh.

Linda's expression remained unamused. "I would've thought you got yourself a boyfriend if I didn't know what a miserable sadist you are. So I'm thinking it's more likely that you started the transitioning process."

"You're right about me not having a boyfriend," Blake said. She finished loading the clothes and turned on the washer.

Then she plopped down on a nearby chair, raising her voice so Linda could hear her over the noise. "The sex change does seem like the more likely option. If things go as planned, I'm hoping to have as much facial hair as you by winter."

"Well, you're already a dick, so I'm sure it won't be long before you *have* one too."

Blake couldn't contain her smile this time, so she kept her head down where it had been directed at the phone on her lap. Over the course of the next half hour or so, Linda had to answer the phone twice and open the vending machine for someone when it didn't give them the soda they'd paid for. It was the most Blake had seen the woman work since she'd started coming here over a year ago.

"I almost didn't recognize you without that stool stuck to your ass," Blake said as Linda returned to her place behind the counter.

"Yeah, well, I'm sure it's better than what you've got stuck to yours most of the time."

Blake thought about asking Linda to explain her comment if for no other reason than entertainment value, but she decided against it. Listening to Linda talk about semen was not on the list of things Blake wanted to accomplish today. Moving the clothing from the washer to the dryer, Blake wondered if there was anything of Gavin's that shouldn't go in there, but she figured if he hadn't given her specific instructions, then whatever she did was fine. She tossed the last of their things into the two machines and turned them on.

"So you still never told me whose underwear you're washing," Linda said.

Blake looked up from her Twitter feed. "I thought we already established that it was mine?"

"I've decided that can't be the case. You don't look like the type to own underwear."

Blake stared at her blankly for a moment before finally responding. "Okay, that was a good one."

But before Linda could reply, their attention was drawn to the lights flickering and then cutting out completely. The washers slowed, spinning a few more times before stopping completely just as the dryers had.

"What the hell?" Blake said, along with a few other people who were headed to the storefront windows to see if the power was out anywhere else.

"Looks like the whole street's out," said one man.

"You have a generator or anything, Linda, in case it doesn't come back on soon?" Blake asked her.

"This isn't a hospital. It's a laundromat."

"Well, what are we supposed to do with our wet clothes?"

"You can leave them here, and I'll finish 'em up for you as soon as we have electricity. But it'll cost you something just like it would if you dropped them off for me to wash and fold."

"Listen, Linda." Blake had been waiting months for the perfect opportunity to say that, and she wondered if the woman even got the reference. "I'm not paying for that. I already paid to wash and dry my stuff. It's not my fault the power went out."

Linda shrugged. "Not my fault either."

Blake sighed as she opened the dryer and began throwing the damp clothing into the big trash bag. She wondered if it would even hold the weight without breaking as she hauled them to the other laundromat. "I'll dry them somewhere else," she said.

"Power's out for blocks," someone chimed in. "My friend just texted."

Blake looked at the bag of clothes and then back to the young man who had just spoken. "I'll figure something out," she said. "I always do."

CHAPTER SIXTEEN

Gavin put the last of the equipment into the company van and shut the doors before taking a look at his watch. It was just after six thirty in the evening, and he'd spent the majority of his day trying to make babies laugh and getting toddlers to sit still. He was amazed at how easily the teachers at the daycare were able to block out distractions when he could barely focus long enough to snap a quick picture of a three-year-old in a fedora. When he'd taken the picture, he'd wondered why anyone would want to preserve such an image but decided not to ask when the boy's parents showed up and began selecting photos like they were creating a wedding album for the kid.

How Gavin's life had veered so far off course that he was taking pictures of kids named after clothing, he couldn't figure out. But there he was, spending his nine-to-five telling children named Denim and Cargo to say cheese. He was thankful when the last few parents had finalized their orders of their child's school portraits on the studio's touchscreens that they'd set up in the lobby of the childcare center. Even though there was a coffee shop next door, there wasn't enough caffeine in the world to make Gavin stay there any longer. He was beat and it was only Monday.

When they got back to the studio, he and Anton unloaded

the van and locked up all the equipment before heading out to the parking lot. At least the weather had gotten considerably better than it'd been over the weekend and even that morning.

"I'll see you later in the week," Gavin said. "I don't think I'm back in until Friday for senior portraits. What about you? You working all week?"

"I've got off Tuesday and Thursday, but then I'm in every day through Sunday, I think."

"All right, man. Take it easy."

"You too," Anton said before getting into his old Nissan and pulling out of the lot.

The ride home was quicker than Gavin had expected it to be, probably because it was after rush hour. As he ascended the three flights of stairs to his apartment, all he could think about was taking a long shower and relaxing on the couch for the rest of the night. He unlocked the door and called, "Hi, honey. I'm home," before grabbing a bottle of water from the fridge and heading toward his room. "Blake? You here? You wanna watch a movie or something and order some food, or did you eat already?"

He figured since her door to her room was shut that she was probably in there, and he hoped he didn't wake her up from a nap or something. Deciding not to knock, he put his ear up to the door to see if he could hear anything. But he almost fell through the threshold when Blake pulled open the flimsy door.

"Jesus," she said. "You scared the hell out of me. I didn't even realize you were home."

"Sorry. I was calling you. You didn't hear me?"

"No. I just came inside. I was out on the fire escape."

Gavin was confused. "Why?"

"Because I was done out there."

"No, why were you out there to begin with?" he asked.

"Oh. I was bringing some stuff in off the line."

"What line? What are you talking about?" he asked, growing even more confused.

"Our clothesline," she said. "We have one now."

"What? Why? I thought you were going to the laundromat to wash some stuff. They have dryers there, you know."

"That I do know. But dryers don't work if the power is off, and the power went off a little after our stuff went in, so I had to improvise."

"Oh, um...okay. You didn't have to do all that, but thanks," he said.

"I had to dry them *some*how. They would've smelled like mildew unless we washed them all over again, and that's a waste of time and money—two things neither one of us has to spare."

Gavin had been wondering how she'd managed to rig up any kind of line to their apartment building, but he figured there was no way to know without asking. "What did you attach it to? There's only one fire escape in our apartment."

"Come on," she said, gesturing for him to follow her into her room and out the window. Once outside, she pointed to the rope she had strung from their fire escape railing to another, two apartments away. "Mrs. Michael let me tie it to hers. It would've been way too short if I attached it to Baby and Guy's fire escape. Plus, that would've involved asking them, and they were yelling about Christmas dinner...and it's only October. I didn't want to get involved," she explained.

"So I threw it to Mrs. Michael, and we lowered it under Baby and Guy's fire escape. You have to be careful that the clothes don't rub against the metal when you pull the string, but otherwise it works perfectly." She crossed her arms and smiled, clearly proud of herself. "There still wasn't enough line to fit everything, so I dried all our heavier stuff first, like jeans and things, and I laid the other stuff around the apartment on towels to dry a little until it was their turn," she said, like the clothing was waiting in line for an amusement park ride. "The first batch is done, and I just put the other things on maybe two hours ago."

Gavin looked down at the sagging rope, which had clothing attached to it with hair clips and bobby pins. "By 'other things,' you mean all my underwear?" he said as he stared at his boxers blowing in the breeze. One pair even had a hole in them that he hadn't noticed until now.

"Yeah. And mine too," she said, pulling on the line so Gavin could see where the small pieces of lace were hung just below Baby and Guy's fire escape.

"So our neighbors have been looking at our underwear all day long?"

"No. I told you. It's only been out there like two hours. And what does it matter anyway?"

"I don't know," he answered. "Doesn't it make you feel weird that people might be eating dinner to the sight of your red thong?"

"No," she said as if the question had been ridiculous. "It's not like their view was that spectacular *before* that. They were probably thankful for the change in scenery."

Gavin shook his head, but somehow he couldn't help but be captivated by the woman in front of him. She was so carefree and unapologetic. He let the smile he felt coming sweep across his face. "You're insane, you know that?"

She smiled back, a gleam in her eyes that he'd come to know well. "So I've been told."

◆ ◆ ◆ ◆

Blake finished her fourth slice of pizza and tossed the crust back into the box on the coffee table in front of them. "I'm stuffed," she said, making Gavin wonder where she put it all. Blake wasn't embarrassed to eat real food in front of him, which was a welcome change from some of the other women he'd dated.

Though what he and Blake had going couldn't exactly be called dating. They worked together, lived together, and slept together. It seemed more of a relationship of convenience than anything else. Though that thought made him more disappointed than he wanted to admit.

"So what's new with the American youth these days?" she asked. "You see any kids with full sleeves of tattoos or baby bumps or anything?"

Gavin laughed out loud at the thought. "Nah, not today. I was at a daycare, remember?"

"Yeah, I remembered. So what?"

"I probably would've had to report that to the authorities if I'd seen either of those things. Unfortunately, the weirdest thing I saw was the kids' names."

"Oh yeah? Like what?"

"They're all named after places. And fabrics," he added. "Like Tennessee or Paisley or something. One kid was named Jupiter. You believe that shit? Who the fuck names their baby Jupiter?"

"That's pretty horrible," Blake admitted. "Still better than Uranus though."

Gavin nearly spit out the beer he'd taken a sip of, but he managed to finish swallowing. "Yes. Jupiter's definitely better than Uranus." He grabbed another piece of pizza and plopped it on his plate. "I swear, if I ever have kids, I'm not naming them anything weird. It's just setting them up for a lifetime of torture. I mean, who's calling someone named Cargo in for an interview when they see his name on a resume?"

"There was a kid named Cargo?"

Gavin nodded. "Yup."

"Man, and I thought *my* name was bad."

"Blake?" Gavin asked. "What's wrong with your name? I like it."

"Yeah. So did my dad. He was convinced I was going to be a boy and refused to change the name he had picked out for his son. I guess I should be thankful he didn't choose something even *more* masculine." She thought for a moment. "I could've been Christopher or Henry or something, I guess."

"Ha! No offense, but I'm not sure I could've slept with you if your name was Henry," Gavin said. He adjusted his position on the couch so he was leaning against the arm of it facing her fully. He was aware that she'd mentioned her father, but something told him not to ask any more about her family. If she wanted to tell him, she would. Besides, he'd been wondering something for a while now, and hadn't ever asked her. But now seemed like as good a time as any. "Can I ask you something?"

"You can always ask," she said. "Though I might choose not to answer."

"Fair enough," Gavin said. And then, "Why don't you have any tattoos?"

"What made you think of that?"

Gavin shrugged. "I thought of it a few minutes ago when you mentioned kids having sleeves of them. But to be honest, I've been curious about it since I met you actually."

She looked surprised.

"Don't take this the wrong way, but you seem like someone who'd have some. You dress the way you wanna dress, say what you wanna say. I guess I just figured you'd express yourself through art too. I was surprised when I saw you naked for the first time that you didn't have any."

"You don't have any either," she pointed out.

"Yeah, but I'm nowhere near as interesting as you. If I ever got one, it'd be something lame, I'm sure. And then I'd have it on me for the rest of my life. I can't commit to something like that."

Blake smiled in a way that made Gavin wonder what was underneath it. Like she wasn't completely there in that moment with him. "My reason for not having any is pretty similar to yours actually," she said.

"Oh yeah? You scared you'll get a tattoo of Super Mario or something?" he asked with a laugh.

"Nah. Doesn't matter what I'd get. The thought that it would be permanent is enough to make me never do it."

"I'm surprised. You don't strike me as the type of person to have many regrets."

"I don't," she said casually. "I try to take life as it comes and make the best of it, but I don't particularly want a permanent reminder of shit inked on my body either." She groaned as if she were annoyed with herself. "I don't know why I keep doing this."

"Doing what?" he asked.

"Sharing shit with you that I don't tell anyone."

"Blake, you don't have to share anything with me that you don't want to share. Remember? Just because I asked the question doesn't mean you have to answer it. You said it yourself."

"I know I don't *have* to," she said. "I'm angry with myself that I *want* to."

CHAPTER SEVENTEEN

Blake wasn't familiar with this feeling—the one that caused her to want to open up to this beautiful, caring man in front of her. Of all the times she'd shared her past with someone, most of them had felt forced. And *all* of them had been with mental health professionals who were being paid to listen to her story, analyze all the ways she was broken, and tell her what she could do to try to fix it.

But here was this guy who she'd met at some random job, and he wanted to know her story, wanted to know *her*. And as much as she tried, she couldn't resist the urge to tell him, as if letting all her shit out into the world would somehow relieve her of some of its weight. "There hasn't been much in my life that's been permanent," she began. "Houses, family, friends, towns...roommates," she said with a low smile. "They've all disappeared almost as quickly as they've come." She thought back to all the houses she'd lived in, the communities she'd passed through. They were all a blur in her mind, like a morning fog that still hadn't been lifted hours into the day. "Nothing in my life has ever lasted long enough to mean anything," she continued. "I lived in seven different houses and two foster homes by the time I was thirteen. At first, the change was tough on me. But eventually it became nothing for me to pack up and move with barely any warning. I got good at it. I'd pretend I was a firefighter responding to a call. It was like a game that way. I'd get dressed, pack up all my gear, and leave without much thought to if I'd ever be back."

She sighed deeply, realizing that she'd let all of that out in almost one breath. Gavin didn't say anything as he waited for her to continue. "I never had pictures or posters on the wall I needed to remember to take with me when I left. I guess I thought if there wasn't any evidence I'd ever been there, it would almost be like I hadn't."

"I'm sorry. You didn't deserve that," he said quietly.

"There isn't anything for you to be sorry about. There isn't anything for *anyone* to be sorry about. Shitty things happen to good people all the time. But I guess that's the reason I don't want a tattoo. I'm so used to things changing, I can't imagine having something that doesn't."

Gavin pressed his lips together and narrowed his eyes. "But you made this space your own now and decorated it with things that you like," Gavin said, gesturing to their surroundings where she had endless trinkets that had taken her years to accumulate. "Wouldn't your body be the same?"

Blake was silent as she thought about Gavin's question. *She'd* always been the one who had to change, the one who had to adapt to whatever hand life dealt her. That flexibility was one of the traits she liked about herself. She couldn't wrap her brain around the present Blake making a decision for the future one. "I guess the difference is that if I don't like some little figurine or candle or something, I can throw it out. I can change the paint color or furniture or whatever if I want to, but a tattoo's forever. There's no erasing it or tossing it in the trash if I get sick of it. I guess I like to keep my options open."

Gavin nodded. "That makes a lot of sense actually," he said. And then, "What made you choose this coral? For the wall color," he clarified.

"It's pretty," she answered so easily it surprised her. "So much of my life has been filled with ugliness that I guess I wanted to be surrounded by beauty for once." Blake couldn't remember the last time she'd cried, but she was damn close to it right now, and the acknowledgment only made it that much more difficult to hold back the tears. She swallowed hard, feeling the lump sting her throat as it slid down.

"What made you change up the color in your room?"

"I read somewhere that blue is calming, so I decided to try it out."

"Does it work?"

"I think so," she said with a shrug. She wasn't sure if it was the wall color or the fact that it was her own space, but she did feel relaxed in her room.

"Why'd you leave the one wall in your bedroom white?" he asked.

It was a good question, but it was one she wasn't sure she was ready to answer. She thought for a moment before deciding that she'd already revealed so much to him, she didn't think she was capable of holding anything back. "I haven't seen my parents since I was fifteen," she said. "And I haven't lived with them since I was seven. They both went to jail for possession a few times when I was young enough that I don't really remember it. But when their addictions got worse, so did their sentences. Eventually they both went away for robbery and some other, more minor charges. But because of their criminal history, it was safe to say they weren't getting out anytime soon."

Blake looked up from where she'd been picking at a piece of her cuticle. Gavin's eyes were on her as he seemed to be listening to every word, unsure of what to say. "Is this too much?" she asked.

He shook his head. "No. No," he said quietly. "I'm glad you're telling me."

And so was she. Blake continued, explaining how the last good memory she had was of her little house in Oak Ridge where she and her parents lived until she was seven and things started to get bad. It wasn't the biggest house or the nicest. But it was *her* house—the last place that truly felt like home to her. "When I was little, I used to be scared of *bad guys*. They'd shown us some stranger-danger type of presentation at school, and I was terrified that someone was going to come in the house and go into my room and take me when I was sleeping. I was scared that I'd wake up and be in some new, unfamiliar place with people I didn't know." She almost laughed at the irony of it. Her fear had come true once she'd been bounced around to various foster homes. But it hadn't been the bad guys who'd taken her; it'd been the *good* ones.

"I'd have dreams that people kidnapped me, and I'd wake up screaming and thinking I was somewhere else. My parents would run in and try to calm me down so I'd stop yelling."

"Is that what you have nightmares about now?" Gavin asked. Though she'd shared so much already, he still looked hesitant to ask more.

"Sometimes," she answered, deciding now wasn't the time to get into the other reason for her bad dreams. "Anyway, one night, my mom told me to put my hand on the wall next to my bed. She ran my hand along it and told me to feel the crack in the plaster. She told me to memorize its shape and path so that when I got scared and thought I was somewhere else, I could just to reach up and touch it so I'd know I was home in my bed. It was just a dirty white wall with a crack in it, but it got me through a lot of nights." She breathed deeply before continuing. "So when I got this apartment and saw there was a similar crack in the bedroom, I couldn't bring myself to paint over it. Guess the chipped white wall looked pretty to me too," she said, thinking it was one of the last good memories she had of her parents. "It feels stupid because that happened almost twenty years ago, but in some ways it still feels like yesterday."

Gavin reached his hand out, placing it on hers without looking away from her. She concentrated on the way his thumb rubbed circles over the back of her hand. The motion soothed her, though she wasn't aware she needed soothing until then. "It's not stupid at all," Gavin said, and somehow the words comforted her a bit. "Tons of people hang on to memories from when they were little."

She smiled, but it was tight against her lips. "Yeah," she said. "But I'm not one of them. Or at least I didn't *think* I was."

◆ ◆ ◆ ◆

Gavin had been practically speechless as Blake told him about her childhood, but somehow he'd been able to ask a few questions—questions she'd trusted him enough to answer. There was no way he could sit silently and listen to everything she'd told him without wanting to know more. It amazed him that the beautiful woman sitting in front of him had been through so much at such a young age. He'd never known anyone who had dealt with as much as she had.

"What are you thinking?" Blake asked him, making him realize that he'd probably been quiet for a bit too long.

"That you're incredible," he said. And he meant it.

"I'm definitely not," she replied, and he thought he saw her cheeks blush a little.

"You definitely *are*," he said again. He let out a deep breath before speaking again. "My parents kicked me out of the house when I refused to follow the path they laid out for me. I wanted to be a photographer, but that wasn't good enough for them. And all this time, I felt like I'd gotten such a raw fucking deal. But here you are, dealing with way worse shit and being strong as hell about it. I pretty much feel like a huge pussy right now."

Blake laughed softly, moving closer to him so she could reach up and touch the back of his neck. His blond curls were soft against her hand as she scratched his scalp lightly with her nails. "You're not a huge pussy," she assured him. And then, "You're like a little one. Medium-sized at most," she said with a smile.

He loved how she had a way of breaking the tension when he needed it, like she knew exactly what to say and when to say it to make him feel at ease. But he was the one who should be doing that for her, not the other way around. "I want you to know how much it means that you told me all that," he said.

"I promise I won't say anything to anyone. You don't have to worry about that."

"I don't. I trust you," she said, leaning in to place a soft kiss on his lips.

Like every other kiss between them, it had a way of leading to more, and in seconds they were tearing off each other's clothing until there was nothing that came between them. Suddenly Gavin was aware of all of her—the thumping of her heart under his chest as they moved together, how perfectly he fit inside her, the smell of her hair as he breathed in her mint and citrus scent.

He worked his hands over her body wildly like he couldn't get enough of her, and he realized it was because he couldn't. This girl, this *woman* beneath him had a hold on him like no one he'd ever encountered before. He couldn't take his eyes off her as his cock thrust inside her, silently begging her to find her release so he could too.

Every breath was a gasp, choppy and labored as he struggled to hold off. But he could sense how close she was by the flush on her neck and chest and the way her eyelids seemed to flutter open for a moment and then close tightly again. "Come on," Gavin said. "I'm right there." And he heard how strained his words sounded. His cock jerked with the need to come, but he slowed his hips a bit to last.

Now his drives were slower, more rhythmic, but no less pleasurable. Every push inside her felt like it could be the one to make him explode, and he gripped the base of his shaft for a few moments to stop himself before moving his fingers to Blake's clit and massaging it.

"Blake, I can't... God, you're so fucking warm...and so wet. Christ," he said, knowing if she didn't come soon he'd have no choice but to stop moving until he could gain control of himself again. "I can't wait much longer."

With those words, he had Blake tumbling over the edge, her body pulsing around his as she told him to let go inside her. He didn't even have time to process her words before his orgasm was there, his cock jerking against her slick walls until he'd emptied himself completely.

He wanted to stay here, wrapped in her warmth with the evidence of their encounter between them. But eventually he pulled out of her, allowing her to get up and head to the bathroom while he picked up his clothes to get dressed.

A few minutes later, Blake returned, wearing nothing but black lace panties and a tight T-shirt that came just above her underwear. When she sat next to him, he pulled her closer, running his hand along her arm as she snuggled into his chest. For a fleeting moment, it crossed his mind that he could stay like this forever, with Blake in his arms. But if he'd learned anything from their conversation, it was that nothing in her life was permanent. And that, unfortunately, included him.

CHAPTER EIGHTEEN

As Blake stole another glance at Gavin, who'd been restocking the napkins, straws, and plastic utensils quietly for the past ten minutes or so, she wondered what was up with him. She couldn't put her finger on whatever emotions he seemed to have swirling inside him, but there was something about how close they'd gotten since he'd moved in that let her know he wasn't himself.

Whether it was sadness or anger or frustration, she wasn't sure, and he hadn't said much to her all morning to give her any indication of what exactly was wrong. She knew what it was like to deal with something internally, to want to be alone in her own head and hope that no one asked her what her problem was. Because false concern was always the worst kind. She knew from experience.

But her concern for Gavin was real—almost tangible—and it made it impossible for her to ignore the way his shoulders slumped as he filled the last of the napkin holders and leaned against the counter. He stared ahead blankly at the stainless-steel cooler where they kept the milk and cream. His mind was somewhere, but it wasn't here. "You all right?" she asked, figuring it was the least invasive of the possible questions she could think of. She also figured that she'd wait to hear his response before deciding whether to press further.

Gavin jerked his head up like she'd startled him, which only confirmed that his thoughts were elsewhere. "Yeah, just thinking," he answered. His tone was surprisingly light, and it made her wonder if he'd made a conscious choice to sound that way.

"It wasn't about whether we should bang in Stu's office while he's at lunch, was it? Because the answer's no. There's no door, his desk and chair are gross, and I'm scared I'll get splinters from the wood paneling on the wall."

Thankfully, Gavin laughed. "Guess the floor's out too then."

"That goes without saying."

"Figured," he said. "And to answer your question, no, I wasn't thinking about having sex in Stu's office...at least until you mentioned it."

"Not gonna happen," she said before hopping up to sit on the counter. "So what *were* you thinking about then?"

"My parents," he said through a groan. "Sorry. It's stupid. I shouldn't be complaining to you about this."

She knew Gavin's hesitance to discuss his relationship with his parents probably came from everything he'd learned about hers the other day, and she didn't want him to feel like his problems weren't important. "If you can't complain to your roommate slash coworker slash lover about it, then who *can* you complain to?"

Gavin seemed to be studying her as if he were trying to figure out if the words were only words or if they were genuine. She hoped her expression told him she really did want to know what was happening. He was quiet a few more seconds before Blake noticed his shoulders sag a bit.

"My dad called the other day and said they'd be in the neighborhood next weekend, and they want to stop by. That's code for 'checking to make sure I'm not squatting in a crack den,' or even worse in their eyes, working some menial job with no future in sight. I don't feel like dealing with it."

"Okay," Blake said, dragging out the word. "I know our apartment isn't a penthouse, but it's not a crack den either."

"It's not that. I don't care what they think of where I live anyway. But for some reason, I do still care what they think of *me*. They're gonna ask a million questions about my life and where it's headed, and none of my answers are ones they wanna hear."

It crossed Blake's mind to suggest that Gavin lie, but she figured if he hadn't decided to do that already, there was probably a reason he was against it. Like he had a heart and a conscience. "It's not like you're living under a bridge swapping blowjobs for food stamps. You're working hard, and you have a place to live. What more do they want?" It occurred to Blake that the answer was probably "a lot more," but she let her question stand.

"I don't know. But my current status definitely isn't anything to brag about. Even I know that. Nothing's changed since the last time I've seen them. Well, except that my old roommate used my rent money to get high, so I had to move, but I doubt that'll impress them," Gavin said dryly.

"What *will*?"

"Huh?" he asked.

"You said that your current situation won't impress them, so what will?"

His eyebrows pressed together in thought, and then he shook his head and shrugged. "I don't know. It's not like they expect me to suddenly have some hotshot career making six figures. But you know they hate the photography thing—"

"What do they hate about it exactly?" Blake hadn't meant to cut him off, but she needed to know the answer. Gavin was quiet for a moment because a woman had come to the counter to place an order. Blake rung her up and told her her order would be up shortly. Then she turned back to Gavin, who was putting a bagel in the toaster.

"Pretty much everything," he said. "The fact that it's an art, that there aren't many jobs that pay well, how subjective the field is. I think the main thing is that they know it's tough to make a living at it."

"Is it?" Blake had no idea.

"Yeah. Seems like it. Unless you work for a company, you'd be an independent contractor or have to start your own business. And that's gotta take a while to get going."

Blake nodded slowly. "Yeah. Probably. What do you ultimately want to do with it?"

"I don't know... I always thought it'd be cool to have my work in a gallery or something to sell, but that's a long way off. And that's even more difficult to make money from. For now, I'd settle for doing some small photo shoots with families or working weddings or something."

"Have you tried seeing what other opportunities there are? Even if you got a job here and there helping out another photographer, it would probably help with networking and getting your work out there for the public to see. It's not much, but it might open some doors in the long run."

"I haven't looked in a few years. I got busy with the jobs I had and couldn't really find the time to look for something better."

"I bet if you were at least actively looking for something, they might support it more. It can't hurt, at least. I mean, I know they'll still think you'll never make a good living from it, but you'll prove them right if you never even try." Gavin opened his mouth to speak, but Blake continued, "That sounded worse than how I meant it. I mean...I'm not saying you aren't trying. The school picture place pays the bills, but I'm guessing anyone who knows how to work a camera can do that. Taking yearbook pictures of pimply teenagers named Kansas isn't exactly showing off your creativity."

Gavin's laugh was enough of a confirmation that she was correct.

"Have you sent your portfolio out to other photographers who might need an assistant or tried putting up some ads online or anything? Maybe you could book a few private shoots?"

Gavin seemed to hesitate. "No. Um... I don't exactly have a portfolio."

Blake tried to temper her shock, but she felt her eyes widen anyway. This was a man with passion, but he didn't seem to be making much of an effort to further his career.

"Well, I *have* one," he said, probably sensing her surprise. "Or *part* of one. But it's like six years old. No one's gonna want to look at that. It doesn't even show the caliber of what I'm capable of now."

Blake smiled a slow and thoughtful grin that she hoped was as enigmatic as it felt. "Then let's find out what you're capable of."

◆ ◆ ◆ ◆

Gavin had never been someone who liked surprises. He wasn't someone who wanted to show up to a place on his birthday and have everyone jump out from behind the furniture. He never took a test without knowing what to study. And he certainly didn't want to go to his own photo shoot unprepared. But when Blake had suggested Gavin take some pictures to start getting a portfolio together prior to his parents' visit, she'd been tight-lipped about what exactly he'd be photographing today, and he wasn't sure why.

She'd told him she'd arrange a few opportunities for him to get some good shots in, and so far, she'd come through. She'd shared the ideas for the first two sessions as soon as she'd been able to secure the details. Somehow she'd managed to find a wedding for him to shoot. The fact that it was outdoors and had other photographers there only confirmed his suspicions that Blake and Gavin probably shouldn't be there, but what he didn't know for sure couldn't hurt him.

Still, he figured the less that could be seen of people's faces, the better. So he concentrated on taking some more artistic shots—flowers in the bride's hand, the interlocked fingers of the bride and groom as they stood at the altar. He even got an adorable picture of the ring bearer pulling the one-year-old flower girl down the aisle in a red wagon. The fact that the photo was from behind didn't stop Blake from warning him to be careful taking pictures of minors. He'd suggested they leave after that comment, and though he wanted to kill Blake for putting him in a situation that resulted in him having pictures of children without their parents' consent, he couldn't help but be appreciative of what she'd potentially risked to help him.

When she'd told him about the infant photo shoot she'd lined up a few days later, he'd been skeptical until she'd assured him the parents did in fact know her and did in fact invite Gavin to take pictures of their newborn for his portfolio as long as he promised to give them a CD that they could use to print their own pictures. It was more than a fair deal, and Gavin was grateful for their help.

But now he had no idea what Blake had in store, and it scared the hell out of him. "You thought it was no big deal to crash a wedding, but you won't even tell me where we're going this time? I feel like I should be worried." He noticed her trying to bite back a grin. "Correction. I *am* worried."

"We're not going anywhere."

"So is someone coming here?" he asked, looking around at the cluttered apartment and thinking he should probably start cleaning it.

She shook her head.

"So then what am I photographing?"

This time she let herself smile. But it was small, and for the first time since he'd met Blake, she looked shy. "Me."

"What? Really?" Blake didn't strike him as someone who would want to pose for pictures. He didn't think he'd ever even seen her take a selfie.

"Yes. Really." Her voice was soft, slow as she seemed to glide toward the couch and lie on her side there. "I want you to draw me like one of your French girls."

Gavin's eyes were the only thing that moved as they darted around the room like the walls were going to tell him what the hell that comment meant. Finally his gaze settled back on her. "What does that mean?"

She rolled her eyes and laughed. "Haven't you ever seen *Titanic*?"

"No."

"And you've never wondered about those memes with that quote and weirdos posing in provocative positions?"

"The only weirdo I've seen posing in a provocative position lately is you."

That earned him a pillow to the chest.

"Are you serious though?" he asked. "You don't need to do that."

"No, I don't," she said, her eyes blazing into his from across the room. "But I want to. I'm yours for the day. Take pictures of anything you want. Though I don't have much planned, so I'm not sure how interesting it'll be. But I figured that would allow you to be creative."

Gavin wanted to tell Blake there was nothing about her that *wasn't* interesting, but he was too excited to speak. Blake was beautiful and captivating. No lens on earth would show her in any other way. After flipping through a million possible photos ideas in his mind, Gavin was finally able to mutter a "Thank you" before heading into his room to grab his bag.

He'd promised to be a fly on the wall during Blake's day and told her it would be best if she went about her business as if he wasn't even there and to let him do the rest. Candid shots were his favorite anyway because they captured a person's essence completely in a single moment. It was what he'd always loved best about photography. In a world that rushed by too fast for anyone to appreciate it, photos allowed time to stand still. They gave people the ability to return to those moments--a child's first smile, a vacation to the Grand Canyon, a holiday they didn't know would be their last with a loved one.

Photos were memories compressed into a tangible object that people could hang onto forever. And in a society where the present never seemed quite as important as the future, being able to hold one moment in time felt almost magical. And for the first time in a long time, watching Blake brought that magic back to him.

It was hidden in a faint smile as she read a book on the fire escape, or in her eyes as she caught a glimpse of him from where she'd propped herself up on one elbow and leaned over the counter to eat a bowl of cereal. And after only two hours of snapping pictures of Blake, he knew he couldn't be that fly on the wall anymore. He needed to be involved in whatever she was doing, needed to be a part of the magic he saw in her. "Let's go out," he said suddenly, making Blake's head jerk up from where she'd been flipping through a magazine.

"You bored with me already?" she teased.

"The opposite, actually. I don't like only watching you when I could be doing something with you instead."

"Oooh, okay. I can think of a few things here we can do." He was sure the desire in her eyes was intentional.

"I'm not sure you'll let me use my camera for that. Though if you're up for it—"

"No way am I helping you make a porn portfolio."

Gavin let out a loud laugh. "So I guess we're going out then."

"Where do you want to go?"

"Anywhere. Doesn't matter."

"'Kay," she said before putting her bowl in the sink. "Let me grab my bag."

CHAPTER NINETEEN

When Blake had first thought of letting Gavin photograph her, the idea had caused her a small amount of anxiety. She didn't love getting her picture taken to begin with, and having someone follow her around with that as their sole purpose sounded even less appealing. But after the first two sessions, she wanted to give Gavin the chance to have unlimited access to something. Or some*one*. And the only person she figured she could convince was herself.

But despite her initial hesitance, being the subject of Gavin's photos had felt easy, natural even. He'd taken most of the pictures before they'd left the apartment, and then a few more on their walk to the ice cream place. She wondered how Gavin would make photos like the ones he'd taken interesting, but she was confident that he could. He'd shown her some of his old portfolio, and she genuinely liked his work. He had a way of bringing life to still images.

Gavin put down his camera while they ate their ice cream cones at a small wrought-iron table on the sidewalk outside of What's the Scoop. They talked about everything, from why the man walking past them in shorts was wearing two different dress socks, to which ice cream flavor they would choose if they could only eat one for the rest of their lives.

"Mint chocolate chip," Gavin said. "Hands down. Not even a competition."

"No way. Mint chocolate chip is too limiting. Vanilla goes with anything. Apple pie, banana milkshakes, birthday cake. It's the multitasker of desserts."

He seemed to think for a second or two before admitting that it was a solid point. "How's the salted caramel pretzel?" he asked, gesturing to what was left of her waffle cone, which wasn't much.

"I hated it," she joked. "You want a bite?" She held the cone out to him before waiting for him to respond because she knew he wouldn't turn it down.

"That's so good," he said after finishing the bite he'd taken. "I don't know why I got espresso chip when I work in a coffee shop."

"Because you're a glutton for punishment," she said with a shrug. "It's why you like hanging around me."

Gavin laughed, but his expression grew serious quickly. Blake could feel the change in the air as his eyes focused in on hers. "Being with you is hardly a punishment," he said.

The comment made her smile, and she felt a warmth spread through her body. It definitely wasn't a punishment being with Gavin either.

◆ ◆ ◆ ◆

"You sure you want me here for this?" Blake asked from the kitchen. "I can leave."

"It's your place too. I'm not gonna ask you to leave. That's rude."

"So is keeping me here when your parents are coming. It'll be weird if I hide out in my room when they're here, but if I meet them, it'll be weird because...well, because *I'm* weird."

Gavin wanted to tell her he wanted her there for moral support—that she'd helped him up until now, and he didn't want her to leave him hanging when he needed her the most, but he didn't want her to feel any sort of pressure. Her presence was enough. "You're not weird," was what he finally settled on.

"I'm pretty sure your parents won't agree."

"Well, they don't agree with a lot of what I think, so let's keep the streak alive." He shot her a cheesy smile and pretended he didn't notice her eye roll. "It'll be fine. Pretend you're crashing one of your parties and have to make small talk."

"Gavin, your relationship with them is already strained. If I do something to add to that—"

"You won't." He walked over to where she was standing in the kitchen and took both her hands in his, pulling them up to his mouth to give them a soft kiss. He heard his phone ding, so he reached into his pocket to pull it out. "They're here anyway, so now you have no choice," he said.

"Seriously? I thought they weren't supposed to be here until three."

He shrugged. "They're always early."

"Two *hours* early?"

"I may have told you they were coming later so you wouldn't try to leave before they got here."

She glared at him, but he could tell there wasn't any real anger behind it. "How much later?"

"Two hours," he answered slowly before heading to the door.

"Gavin!" she yelled, but her voice faded quickly as he opened the door.

Gavin gave his parents each a hug and stepped to the side so they could enter. "Come on in," he said. "This is my roommate, Blake."

Blake lifted her arm enough that it could almost be considered a wave. "Nice to meet you, Mr. and Mrs. Gibson."

"Please, call me Gail," his mom said. "And Greg." She nodded toward Gavin's father.

"Gail, Greg, and Gavin Gibson," Blake said. "That's very... alliterative."

His parents nodded awkwardly and moved toward the living room to take a seat while Gavin headed to get drinks from the kitchen. Blake mouthed a "See?" to him and threw up her arms in surrender. He guessed it was because she'd said something she regretted before they'd even had a chance to sit down. He brought out some lemonade and cookies from the kitchen and set everything down on the coffee table before taking a seat in one of the chairs.

"How long have you lived here?" his dad asked after swallowing the bite he'd taken of an oatmeal raisin cookie. His head moved back and forth as he scanned his surroundings, and Gavin was sure he was making internal judgments about the place Gavin had chosen to live. And that meant he was probably also making judgments about Blake. It was a realization Gavin didn't like, but he chose not to go there right now.

"A few months. My old roommate couldn't afford the rent anymore, so we both had to move." It was *close* to the truth. "Blake's roommate had just moved out, so the timing worked out."

"Oh, so you two aren't...seeing each other?" His mother gestured between the two of them.

It crossed Gavin's mind to tell her that if by "seeing each other," she meant seeing each other naked, then yes. Yes, they were seeing each other. He hesitated about how to answer because though they had no title—because a title would mean a commitment—they were certainly more than friends. At least in Gavin's eyes. "We know each other from The Coffee Bean," Gavin offered, hoping that would provide her with enough information to appease her.

Nodding, his mom settled her hands on her lap and leaned back against the couch. "So you haven't found anything more stable?" his mom asked.

"My jobs *are* stable," he said. "I have regular hours and work more than full-time between the coffee shop and the portrait studio." His eyes moved to Blake, who was sitting quietly on the chair as she listened to the conversation. He thought about how awkward this must be for her, and he instantly regretted insisting that she stay. Even though it was nice for him to have her there with him, the decision had been a selfish one.

His dad scoffed, clearly unimpressed by Gavin's answer. "Making lattes and telling kids to say cheese aren't exactly jobs to brag about."

Gavin noticed Blake's eyes on his, widening as they silently urged him to speak up. Gavin was in the process of finishing his portfolio and already had some potential contacts that he was planning to send everything to once it was ready, but suddenly he didn't want to tell his parents all that. Because ultimately, he realized that what he'd done, he'd done to better himself, not to please his parents. For the first time in a long time, he'd enjoyed the photography process itself and was excited about where it might lead him. He wasn't going to let his parents taint that excitement.

Suddenly, he was aware of the other three people staring at him as they waited for him to respond. "I wouldn't be so sure," he said. "I can make one hell of a latte."

The surprise on his father's face was enough to let Gavin know that his comment had served its intended purpose. "Gavin, your life, and what you plan to do with it, isn't a joke to us, and we wish it wouldn't be a joke to you either."

"Who's joking?" Gavin asked. "You should see some of the designs in the foam that I've made."

He didn't miss the slow smile that crept over Blake's face. "He's being ridiculous," Blake said, causing his parents' gazes to shift to her. "His designs are nowhere as detailed as mine." She looked to Gavin. "Remember the time when I drew a dick in that dude's cappuccino?"

No, Gavin did not remember that because it never happened.

"A what?" his mom asked, practically choking on her cookie. She probably wasn't sure that she'd heard Blake right, though Gavin knew she had.

"A dick," Blake said again. "Cock, penis, wang, shlong,

whatever you wanna call it. This guy was being a prick, so I drew one in his drink."

Gavin tried not to smile as he held back a laugh after it dawned on him that Blake was pulling his parents' negative attention her way instead of his.

"So this is what you're focusing on now?" his dad asked. "Drawing pornography on people's food?"

Finally, Gavin schooled his features as his attention went to his father, who clearly didn't find Blake's comment as humorous as Gavin did. "No. That's not what I'm focusing on," he said. "But I've decided that since nothing I've ever focused on has been good enough for you, it's not worth mentioning."

His response seemed to make his parents uneasy as if they hadn't expected him to dismiss them so easily. His father cleared his throat as he seemed to process Gavin's words. "So our opinion is worthless to you then?"

"It's not worthless," Gavin answered. "I wish you supported my goals. But you don't." He shrugged and let the silence hang between them before he spoke again. "And I think I'm finally ready to accept that. I can't let your opinion influence what I do or don't do because, ultimately, I'm the only person who has to live with my decisions."

His mom inhaled deeply like she'd forgotten how to breathe while he was speaking. "I don't quite know what to say," his mom said softly.

"I think, for once, you shouldn't say *anything*," Gavin said. "You either want to have a good relationship with the son you have, or a bad relationship because of the son you don't. I'll let you think about it." And with that, Gavin stood, signaling to his parents that their visit there was coming to an end.

Once the door had closed behind them, Gavin turned to Blake, letting the tension of the moment leave with his mom and dad. "Penis designs? Really?"

Blake simply shrugged. "Told you not to let me stay," she said with a smile.

CHAPTER TWENTY

Blake was tired. A kind of bone-tired that came from closing the bar the night before and having her shift start in the morning at the coffeehouse. Even though it was only about three fifteen in the afternoon when she walked into her apartment, she planned to head right to her room and crash.

On her way through the living room, she saw Gavin sitting on the couch sifting through proofs he had spread out on the coffee table. "Hey," she said.

He jerked his head up like he was startled. "Hey."

"Whatcha doin'?"

"Sorting through pictures to see which would be best to put in my portfolio."

She took a step closer to the table. "Have any favorites?"

Gavin sat back and offered her a small smile. "Well, my absolute favorite one isn't in this pile."

"Where is it?"

"Behind you."

Blake narrowed her eyes at him slightly before spinning around. When her eyes found what he was referring to, her entire body went rigid as her blood seemed to thunder in her ears. Emotions flooded through her system, overloading her senses. There, on her bright coral wall, was a framed picture of them that Gavin must have snapped during the photo shoot. His arm was around her, and their smiles were wide as they looked at each other with affection that was so clear the word might as well have been stamped on them. Since her eyes were on him, she hadn't even realized he'd taken it. It was somehow the most beautiful and most frightening picture Blake had ever seen. Her chest began to heave as her eyes and throat burned. It felt like a panic attack was trying to take hold, but there were so many things at war within her, the panic couldn't quite get a handle on her. Instead, everything seemed to converge into one feeling. Rage.

She whirled around to face him. "What the fuck is that?"

Gavin's face fell quickly, and he immediately sat up straighter. "It's a picture. Of us."

"Yeah, no shit. Why is it on my goddamn wall?"

He looked confused and worried and a little scared. "I thought it would be nice. To have a picture of us in our apartment. We look happy in it."

She stormed over to the small frame and took it off the hook and tossed it onto his lap. Then she pivoted and began hurrying to her room. She had to get away from him. Away from the fucking picture.

But Gavin seemed to be having none of that. "What the fuck, Blake?" he said as he followed her down the hall.

She opened the door to her room and tried to close it in his face, but he put his foot in the doorway to stop it. "Move," she gritted out.

"Not until you tell me what the hell I did wrong? You're acting crazy, even for you." His eyes widened as soon as the words were out of his mouth, clearly surprised he'd let them slip.

His words hit her hard in a way she'd never be able to articulate. Because even though she referred to herself as crazy in jest, it was a whole different thing to have it hurled at her by someone else. But she covered the wound in the way she'd learned as a kid—with barbs. "I'm not acting, Gavin. I *am* crazy. Even spent a bit of time in a mental ward as a child because a few other foster kids at the house we were staying at decided it would be fun to lock me in a closet right before we were supposed to catch the bus to school. I was trapped in there all day because my foster parents assumed everyone got on the bus and then they left for work. I didn't talk much before that happened, but I hardly talked afterward for almost two years and started acting out. I probably would've bounced back faster, but one of the therapists believed that holding children tightly for extended periods would fix their attachment issues. That was a special kind of hell for an eight-year-old who was terrified of confined spaces. You wondered what my nightmares are about? Well, now you know."

Gavin looked sick, but Blake didn't care. He wanted to make judgments about her? Act like he knew her? Well, fuck him. He didn't know shit.

Blake threw open the door and gestured around her room. "Look around, Gavin. What *don't* you see?"

His eyes never wavered from her. "Blake...please."

She wasn't going to let him try to deter her from her point. "Pictures," she answered for him. "Not a single goddamn one." Blake didn't even have any of herself. Offering to let Gavin

183

photograph her had been extraordinarily hard for her. But she'd fought through it because she wanted to help. "Wanna know why?"

He looked wrecked, but so was she. She'd been wrecked for a long time. "The first reason is because I don't have any. My parents were too busy getting high to want to capture any family moments." She said the final two words in a tone that showed how preposterous the notion was. Blake's parents hadn't been entirely terrible people, but they certainly hadn't taken any family vacations or spent quality time together that warranted being immortalized with a photo.

"I don't remember anyone taking pictures of me in foster care unless it was for my file. And as an adult..." Blake swallowed thickly. "I don't need a photographic reminder of the people who come in and out of my life. Because I learned pretty early on that people don't hang around, so why the hell would I hang them on my walls?"

"That's not true though. Not everyone leaves."

"Do you want to know how many foster families I was placed with?" She knew he wouldn't answer, so she barely hesitated before continuing. "Fourteen. And do you know how many of those families told me I could get comfortable? That they wouldn't send me away?" She raised her eyebrows in challenge. "Almost every one of them. And I broke a little bit every time I realized they'd lied until I finally smartened up and stopped letting myself get attached. People come and go. The only one I'm stuck with is myself, so I decided to start taking care of me. I know that might be hard for you to understand since it took you until you were twenty-five to accept, but—"

"What are you talking about? What took me until I was twenty-five to accept?"

"That the only person who should matter in your life, the only person you can count on to be there for you is you. If you think I'm wrong, well, look around. I don't see your parents anywhere." Blake knew she was hitting below the belt with that one, but she couldn't stop the words from coming out before they did. But she was thankful Gavin hadn't chosen to respond to her comment because she regretted saying it as soon as it crossed her lips. She took a breath to try to calm herself before speaking again. "Being whoever the hell I wanted to be without apologizing for anything. That's how I know David Belson. He helped me get emancipated when I was sixteen."

Gavin took a step toward her, but something in her face must have told him to back off because he stopped suddenly. "But you do have people who care about you. There's Celeste. And Emily."

She cut him off before he could add himself to the list, because she was sure he would have, and she couldn't hear it. "I adore those girls, especially Celeste. But they're not vital. If they dropped me tomorrow, I'd miss them, but I'd be okay. I'd understand, and I'd be able to move on without skipping a beat because there's no footprint of them on my life. No shared clothes, no borrowed items—"

"No pictures," Gavin finished for her.

"No pictures." Blake sighed, some of her anger evaporating and resignation setting in. "You're a great guy, Gavin. One of the best I've ever met. But I told you not to try to tie yourself to me. Because this was always how this was going to go." She moved forward and tapped the picture he held in his hands. "I don't do relationships, and I sure as hell don't do memories. So you do whatever you want with that, but I don't ever want to see it again."

With nothing left to say and her room feeling too confining, Blake pushed past Gavin and fled the apartment, knowing she couldn't outrun what had happened but was determined to try anyway.

◆ ◆ ◆ ◆

Gavin stood in her doorway for he didn't even know how long. It felt as though his limbs had been filled with lead. There was no way he could have known a simple gesture like hanging a picture of them would set her off like that.

Could he?

He finally forced himself to move and went back to the living room where he plopped down on the couch, tossed the frame aside, and buried his head in his hands. When he lifted it again, he looked around the room and tried to see it as Blake did. Sure, there was shit around, little trinkets and such, but not a single picture. He'd never even paid that much attention to that fact. He'd noticed it, sure. But as with the closet doors, he'd pushed it aside without really thinking about the why of it.

He picked up the picture and studied it. It was clear what he'd captured. This wasn't a picture of two roommates or even two friends. The way they looked at one another—it was like he'd caught the purest manifestation of love possible between two people. Gavin was sure of how he felt, and he was fairly certain of Blake's feelings as well. He felt like he probably recognized her feelings even though she seemed incapable of seeing them clearly herself.

But how was he supposed to get through to her when everyone she'd loved in her life had abandoned her? He didn't blame her for being guarded. It was a matter of self-preservation. Gavin's parents had always accused him of not being serious about his life, and he'd railed against that accusation at every turn because he sure as hell was serious. Serious about his art, and serious about Blake. The difference was, if he fell out of love with his art, he was the only one who'd be hurt by it. Should he try to get through to her when there were no guarantees they'd work out? When he couldn't promise he wouldn't eventually leave? Just because he couldn't envision it happening didn't mean it wouldn't.

Blake clearly didn't feel like it was worth the risk. And sitting on the couch with his thoughts all over the place, Gavin wasn't sure he disagreed.

CHAPTER TWENTY-ONE

Blake walked. And walked. And walked some more. Her brain was in overdrive, and she couldn't sort through her thoughts enough to get any clarity. She was thankful she'd at least been able to stave off a panic attack. *God, I'm such a mess.*

She eventually found herself standing in front of a park entrance and turned in. She found a bench across from a fountain and sat down, staring at the water as it cascaded from the top tiers. A little girl was standing beside it, throwing change into the water and giggling as her father smiled at her and kept feeding her coins.

It was a Kodak moment if Blake had ever seen one, and it made her want to hurl rocks at them both. Of course, she never *would*. Despite Gavin thinking she was certifiable, she wouldn't actually hurt anyone.

Except evidently him.

There was no doubt about it—Blake knew that her reaction had hurt Gavin. It probably seemed completely over the top to him. No normal person would go ballistic over a cute picture with her boyfriend.

Boyfriend. Was that really how she thought of Gavin? When had that happened?

Despite the walls she'd built to fortify her for a lifetime,

Gavin had managed to sneak inside. She hadn't even realized she'd been under siege until she'd seen that picture. And by then it was too late. He was already in, burrowing his way into her like a fucking virus. Even when he left, there would always be a trace of him there. And that...really fucking sucked.

Blake had a lot of issues, but being delusional wasn't one of them. She knew she came with an expiration date. Eventually, she started to grate on people until the relationship went bad and needed to be trashed. Some people had a higher tolerance than others, but the end result was always the same. Why put herself—and him—through that?

She'd warned him. She'd fucking warned him, and the stupid jerk hadn't listened, and now she was mentally berating herself as she scowled at the happiness of a four-year-old because she had reached that level of fucked up. The one thing Blake had always had going for her was that she was unequivocally and unapologetically herself.

So why the hell was she sitting on a bench and wondering who the hell she even was?

Or maybe that wasn't accurate. She wondered who she *wanted* to be. And maybe to answer that, she had to face some harsh truths.

The first was that she'd lied about Celeste. Blake wouldn't be even remotely okay if Celeste stopped talking to her. Maybe Blake had been able to keep the illusion that their lives weren't intertwined, but the truth was the two of them were like sisters. Losing that would cut deep, and Blake knew she'd do everything in her power to make sure that never happened.

Which begged the question, if she was willing to do that

for Celeste, why wasn't she willing to do it for Gavin?

There were reasonable explanations. She hadn't known Gavin as long, so the trust wasn't as ingrained. The nature of their relationship was different since Blake had no interest in seeing Celeste naked, and Celeste was pretty similar to Blake. Gavin was so different. Reserved and kind and gentle and normal. Though he seemed to like Blake a hell of a lot, so maybe he wasn't *completely* normal.

The other truth she needed to face was that, even though she tried to pretend otherwise, Blake longed for human connections. She was lonely—had been for most of her life, though she wasn't sure she realized how much until Gavin came along. Gavin had filled a lot of that void. It would be easy to depend on that, and Blake didn't do dependence. That had gotten her hurt more than almost anything else in her life.

But as she took stock of the ache in her chest and the gritty feeling in her throat, she wondered if it could really hurt any more than it did after walking out on Gavin.

Gavin.

At the thought of his name, an image popped into her mind. His blond hair that he sometimes let grow out a little too long so it curled around his ears, his square jaw that always looked biteable in the mornings when stubble dotted it, his solid frame that enveloped her and made her feel safe.

A few stray tears escaped Blake's eyes as the realization hit her. It didn't matter if she never saw another picture of Gavin in her entire life. His likeness was imprinted on her brain. And it would always be there for the insanely complicated fact that she loved him. She'd probably started falling a little bit in love with him that very first day she'd met him, and it had only grown stronger with every day that had passed since.

And as she continued to sit and watch the water, Blake faced the last truth she needed to confront. She was really fucking dumb.

◆ ◆ ◆ ◆

Gavin stared at his phone, wondering if he should call her or not. He wanted to make sure she was okay, but would hearing from him only keep her away longer? The more time that passed, the more pissed off he got. All this because of a picture. And while he knew it was more than that, deeper, it still irked him that she hadn't even given him a chance to be her friend. If she didn't want more, he'd figure out how to deal with it. But she could've at least been a fucking adult and talked to him about it instead of running away and making him worry.

When he finally heard the door open a few hours after she'd left, he'd worked himself into such a tizzy he nearly leaped off the couch and rushed to confront her. But he needed to keep a calm head. Freaking out wouldn't do the situation any good.

He sat still and waited to see what she was going to do. It took her a minute to come toward him, and when she did so, her gait was slow but steady. They looked at one another for a long moment before she spoke. "So I may have overreacted."

Air whooshed out of him. "Ya think?"

One side of her mouth tilted up slightly. "I never claimed to be rational."

No, no, she didn't.

She stood there and fidgeted with her hands before crossing them. "I'm sorry I said all that stuff."

"I'm not," he countered, which caused surprise to flash across her face. "I needed to hear it. Even if we're never more than friends, I still want to know you, Blake. I want to understand."

She snorted. "That's a really tall order."

Gavin smiled. "Kind of like a grande quad nonfat one-pump no-whip mocha latte?"

That caused her to laugh loudly. "That drink is going to haunt me forever, isn't it?"

Standing slowly, Gavin took measured steps toward her. "Probably. Because I plan to be in your life forever, however you decide to have me."

A smirk started forming on her mouth. "There are lots of ways I want to have you."

That sounded...promising. "Oh yeah?"

"Yeah." Blake let out a breath. "I've forced myself to be okay for so long that I never stopped to ask myself if I was actually happy. And I wasn't. Not until you. And I'm scared to death of losing that, Gavin, but I'm even more afraid of never having it at all."

That was everything he'd needed to hear. Reaching up, he tucked a strand of her hair behind her ear. "You make me happy too."

"I can't promise I won't freak out ever again."

"Just don't run. If you're freaking out, then we'll deal with it. But I can't handle not knowing if you're okay."

She leaned toward him, and their arms wrapped around

each other. "You're too good for me. You know that, right?"

"I think we're good together. Perfect even."

They stood there for a while, and Gavin relished the closeness.

Blake was the first to pull away. "So where's the picture? I want to hang it back up."

"You don't have to do that."

"No, I want to. I need to. I have to work on my issues. Especially the ones that don't make any sense."

Gavin wanted to argue that her issues made total sense, but there was a more concerning problem to deal with first. "I... kind of threw it out."

"What? Why would you do that? I love that picture."

Gavin couldn't help but laugh. "There is literally no one else in the world like you. You know that?"

"Yes, thank God. Now which trash can did you throw it out in?" She didn't wait for him to respond before she went into the kitchen and took the lid off the trash can. A second later, she was back with the frame. She walked over to the hook he'd nailed into place earlier and rehung it. "There. Perfect. Just like you said." Standing in front of the picture, Blake didn't take her eyes off it.

Gavin went to her and slid his hands around her waist as he pressed against her back. "Definitely perfect."

"You look like you love me in that picture," she said, her voice low and clearly fishing.

"That's how I look, huh?"

"Yup."

Gavin squeezed her a little tighter. "And how do you

look?"

Nestling back into him, Blake relaxed her head against his chest. "Like I love you back."

Gavin had spent a lot of his life wondering if he was doing the right things. But there, in that moment with Blake, he was confident he was exactly where he was supposed to be, doing exactly what he was supposed to be doing—loving this girl, his girl, with every fiber of his being. And being loved in return.

CHAPTER TWENTY-TWO

Gavin noticed Blake leaning against the doorway of his room, but he was too busy fixing his hair to turn toward her.

"We're going to be late," she stated plainly.

Ignoring her, Gavin decided his hair was as good as it was going to get and smoothed his hand over his black button-down.

"Shouldn't you *not* be late?" she asked.

"Stop stressing me out," Gavin muttered as he shrugged into his suit jacket and analyzed his reflection. "What do you think of this jacket?"

"I think it's going to be late to its own gallery show."

"Pretty sure the jacket isn't the one having the show," he replied as he took the jacket off.

When she remained quiet, Gavin looked over at her. She was looking at him curiously.

"What?" he asked.

"I think I'm rubbing off on you, and I'm not sure it's a good thing."

"Why? Because I can't make up my mind about what I should wear on the most important night of my life?"

"No, because you're talking about your jacket like it's a person."

Gavin snorted. "You did it first."

He heard her sigh loudly. "Which is exactly my point. I am not your gauge for what's normal, Gavin. You know this."

He decided to forego the jacket, gave himself one more once-over, and walked over to her. Pressing his lips to hers, he gave her a sweet kiss that he hoped held a hint of promise for what was to come later. "Normal is overrated," he said when he pulled back a moment later.

"Yeah, it's also...normal," she said.

That made him smile. "Very eloquent."

"Whatever. I get dumber when you're this close to me because all I can think about is how much I—"

Gavin covered her mouth with his hand, causing her to stop speaking immediately. "Please don't finish that sentence. A hard-on doesn't go with this outfit."

A carnal smile lit up Blake's face. "I disagree. I wish a hard-on would find its way inside my outfit. And my body."

"Jesus Christ," Gavin muttered as he let his eyes rove over the outfit she'd mentioned. She was in a formfitting red wrap dress that hugged her curves and dipped down low enough to show a hint of her ample cleavage. Her hair hung in waves around her shoulders, and her black heels were stilettos. "You look amazing. So we need to hurry up and leave before I decide to skip the show and stay here and fuck you instead."

"How romantic," Blake said through a laugh as she started down the hall.

As they walked past the picture of the two of them hanging on the wall, Blake kissed two of her fingers and pressed them against the glass, as she did every time she left the apartment.

It was something she'd started doing the day after their fight over it. He didn't ask her about it right away because he didn't want to jinx the fondness she clearly had for the photo. But after about a week, curiosity got the best of him.

Her response was simple. She said she loved the people in that picture and always wanted to make sure they knew it. It was odd and quirky and so Blake that Gavin felt like his love for her grew even more. Four months later, and she never forgot to do it.

She'd also let him take a few more pictures of the two of them together, and she'd snapped quite a few on her phone as well, but they hadn't hung any up yet. Blake hadn't asked him to, and he didn't want to push. The one they had displayed was enough for now.

They hurried downstairs and jumped into the Uber they'd requested that had been idling outside for probably close to twenty minutes.

"Sorry for the wait," Gavin said to the driver after they climbed in.

"No worries," the guy replied as he put the car in gear and pulled out into traffic.

Gavin figured it probably didn't matter since he'd have to pay for the time whether the guy was kept waiting or not.

Blake smoothed a hand over his chest. "I really like this whole brooding artist thing you have going."

Gavin looked down at himself. "What do you mean? I'm not brooding."

"You're wearing a black shirt with black pants. It's very dark and mysterious. And the top button being left open ups the hotness factor."

"You don't think I should've worn a tie?" he asked.

"No. Ties are boring. And in this outfit, you are definitely anything but boring."

"So what I'm wearing makes you...excited?"

"I am *dripping* with excitement."

Gavin knew they weren't being nearly as subtle as they hoped, but he couldn't bring himself to care. He stared for a minute at the woman who made him feel brave and strong and so fucking alive he sometimes felt like he would burst from it. "I seriously couldn't love you more."

Blake seemed to startle slightly at his words, but then a slow smile spread across her lips. "Back at ya."

He reached over and laced his fingers with her before settling back into the seat. The drive was fairly quick, and before he knew it, Gavin was standing in front of the gallery that was showing his photographs, as well as some work of a few other artists. He stared up at the building for a couple minutes, trying to take everything in.

Blake didn't say anything. She just stood beside him and shared the moment with him. And he was supremely thankful for that. He'd told his parents about the show. They'd congratulated him in toneless voices that let him know they still found him lacking. And while that sucked, it was also okay. He hadn't done any of this for them. Gavin was proud of himself, even if they weren't.

"I'm ready," he finally whispered.

She squeezed his hand in reply, and they walked into the gallery. The space was fairly large and teeming with people.

While Gavin had hoped the variety of artists would draw a crowd, he hadn't even let himself hope for the kind of turnout that was awaiting him.

As soon as they were in the door, the gallery owner's assistant was on them. "There are already two critics here from the local papers, one from an art magazine, as well as three bloggers with impressive online followings. There are also quite a few big buyers here. They all keep going back to your photos, so get over there and sell your ass off." She gave him a pat on the shoulder that was more of a push.

He only made it a few steps before he froze. This was really happening. He'd put his work out there, and people were actually looking at it, critiquing it, maybe ripping it to shreds. He had so much riding on tonight. This was where he'd see if he really had what it took to make it in this world. *What if I find out I don't?* He'd managed to keep that doubt mostly at bay leading up to the show, but now that he was here, he couldn't deny how much he wanted this—wanted to fit into this world that he'd sacrificed so much to be a part of.

"If you could not literally sell your ass off, that'd be great. I need something to grab onto when you're banging the hell out of me." Blake's words were whispered in his ear and broke through the temporary paralysis he'd succumbed to. She couldn't have said anything more perfect.

"I wouldn't dream of it."

"Good. You can, however, sell *my* ass, since I see it hanging over there."

Gavin looked in the direction of her gesture and saw a picture he'd taken of her in their kitchen. She had been trying to reach a bowl on the top shelf of one of their cabinets and had put her palms on the countertop to hoist herself up. One foot was dangling while her other knee found purchase on the Kama Sutra tiles as she reached up for the bowl with one hand. Her body was elongated elegantly and her auburn hair cascaded beautifully down her back, perfectly illuminated by a ray of sunlight that peeked through the kitchen window. The depth of field made the cabinets slightly out of focus, drawing the eye to Blake in the best possible way.

Gavin had taken hundreds—maybe thousands—of pictures when the gallery had told him they wanted to feature his work after seeing his portfolio. He had walked around for weeks with his camera around his neck searching for inspiration. But he'd found most of it in their apartment. As it turned out, his muse was a foul-mouthed, sex-obsessed, gorgeous woman whom he was crazy about. Of the fifteen images he'd chosen for the show, seven of them were of Blake. He would've put up more of her, but he'd wanted to show that he was capable of taking pictures of more than one subject. His theme was candids, which was vague as hell. He wasn't sure how the gallery owner Siobhan hadn't objected to it, but he was glad since it allowed him to photograph almost anything he came across. And while printing and framing them had been expensive, when he saw them hanging on the wall, perfectly lit and in front of a crowd who seemed to appreciate them, the cost was worth it. He'd worry about how he was going to eat later. For now, he was allowing himself to bask in the moment.

He began to mingle as people came to look at his work. Blake stayed near him but seemed content to let him do his thing while she maintained silent support. There was interest in his work, which was enough for him. He hadn't come in expecting to sell much, if anything, and that was okay. He was in it for the validation. And as much as it surprised him, he was getting it.

As he spoke to a man and woman about where his inspiration had come from, his eyes strayed to Blake. She was watching him, a slight smile on her face, her eyes warm. He knew she was so much more than the inspiration for his art. She was his inspiration to be a better man. And he vowed then and there to never do anything to lose it.

Blake loved watching Gavin in his element. And no matter how nervous he'd been, this was his element. Talking to people about his art was natural for him, despite the fact that Gavin wasn't typically much of a talker. The passion was clear in his tone, and it drew people to him and made them take an interest in his work. Even though by the end of the night, he'd only sold three photographs, he was still on cloud nine. The gallery owner told him three was actually a good showing for an unknown photographer and that there would likely be more in the following weeks.

A few of Gavin's friends, as well as Celeste and Emily, had stopped by to offer support, which Gavin had clearly been touched by. The night wore on, and Blake remained mostly quiet a true feat for her—content to let Gavin mingle and make new friends. But she couldn't lie. When the evening was finally over, Blake was more than ready to go home. Standing around had been oddly exhausting, and as she got into the Uber they'd requested to take them home, Blake sprawled across the back seat, her legs dangling out the door.

"Uh, you going to scoot in so I can sit down, or should I just lie on top of you?" she heard Gavin ask.

Blake was silent as she thought over her options, but her thinking was cut short by the driver firmly stating, "Having sex back there is a hundred dollars extra."

Blake raised up onto her elbows so she could look at the driver. "A hundred? That's all?"

The driver shrugged in reply.

Blake had more questions, but Gavin pushed her feet to the floor, causing the rest of her body to swivel around.

"Don't even think about it," Gavin warned, though his voice was laced with humor.

"Too late. I've been thinking about it since he said it."

Gavin shook his head, but he was smiling. "What am I going to do with you?"

"Well, you're obviously not going to fuck me in the back of this car, so I'm out of ideas," she grumbled.

"You? Out of ideas? I find that highly unlikely."

Blake couldn't suppress her smile. "Maybe I have a few ideas."

"That's my girl." Gavin put his arm around her and pulled her to him. "Thank you," he whispered.

Craning her neck so she could look up at him, she asked, "For what?"

"Everything. Convincing me to get off my ass and give my art a real shot, supporting me at the show, making me happy.

Just everything."

Blake tucked her head under his chin. "I don't think I've ever made anyone happy before." The words were out before she could censor them, as usual. She truly did wish she hadn't said them though. They made the moment too much about her when it was supposed to be all about him.

But Gavin handled it as only he could. "That's because everyone you've met before me is dumb as hell."

A laugh bubbled up as she tried to melt into him. The drive home passed quickly, and Blake couldn't help her own nerves from rearing up. She wanted to do something special for Gavin to celebrate, and she hoped he liked what she'd done.

They walked up to their apartment hand-in-hand, and Gavin moved to open the door, but Blake wanted to be the first inside. She practically bodychecked him out of the way before slipping her key into the lock and pushing the door open. Once they were both inside and the door was closed, Blake turned on a light in the living room.

She heard Gavin suck in a breath behind her, but she was too scared to turn and face him. So she stood rooted to the spot and let him wander around the room and took in the change of decor.

After her initial freak-out over the picture of the two of them, Gavin hadn't hung any others. She knew he was respecting her space and giving her time to acclimate to their relationship. But pictures were Gavin's life, and she didn't want him to compromise that part of himself just to suit her.

Despite the fact that Blake said a lot of words over the course of any given day, she wasn't always the best at getting her meaning across. So she decided to forego words and give Gavin tangible evidence of how she felt about him. How they felt about *each other*. Because as she looked around the room at the various pictures that now hung on every wall in the room—as well as a few in the hall—it was clear that the feelings were mutual.

After a few minutes of looking around, he turned to her. "When did you do this?"

"I had Celeste and Emily hang them while we were at your show. I drew them a map and everything so they'd know what to put where. Celeste bitched about me being a pain in the ass, but it looks like they put each photo where I wanted it."

"I don't...I don't know what to say." Gavin looked stunned, and Blake wasn't sure if it was the good kind.

"If you don't like them, I can—"

Her sentence was cut off by Gavin striding toward her and crashing his mouth down on hers. The kiss was consuming and possessive and carnal, and it made Blake want to climb him like a spider monkey. So she did.

Gavin squeezed her ass through the fabric of her dress as she gyrated against him. She barely registered that they were moving until Gavin plopped down on the couch, still holding onto her tightly. He slid his hands under her dress and groaned. "Did you seriously not have underwear on tonight?"

"This dress is too tight. I would've had panty lines."

"You couldn't be more perfect," he said before he took her lips in a frenzied kiss and all but tore her dress from her body. His hands left her briefly to undo his pants and then were back on her, guiding her to sit on his hard cock.

Blake moved her hands to grab onto the back of the couch as she rode Gavin like her life depended on it.

His hands were all over her as he pumped up into her. The room was filled with moans, whines, and the smacking of flesh as the two of them tried to get as close to one another as possible.

Blake felt her orgasm building all too soon. She wanted this moment between them to last forever—wished she could photograph it and hang it on the wall in her room, which they both now slept in.

Gavin's cock pushed impossibly deep, stretching the walls of her pussy in the most delicious way, and she was a goner, her entire body clenching, causing her to fold over him as he continued to thrust into her.

"Fuck yeah," he muttered before pumping into her twice more and then holding himself inside of her as his release emptied into her. He gave a few more shallow thrusts, his body twitching with his orgasm.

They rested their foreheads against one another's, panting harshly.

Eventually, Blake caught her breath enough to speak. "So I guess that means you like the pictures."

Gavin laughed, and it made his still half-hard cock move inside her, which made the thrill of a round two zip through her. He brought a hand up to cup her cheek and pressed a kiss to her lips. "I love them. And I love you."

"That's good, because you're never getting rid of me."

"You're never getting rid of me either," he replied.

Blake smiled at him before wrapping her arms around

him, reveling in the man who would be her last roommate and the first love of her life.

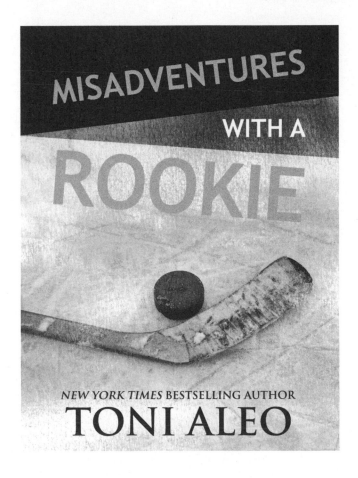

EXCERPT FROM
MISADVENTURES WITH
A ROOKIE

Gus "the Bus" Persson was a showboating, entitled, rich fuck who got on my last nerve. His nickname? Please. *Bus?* He wasn't a bus. He was just a meathead who ran into everyone! Rolling my eyes for the umpteenth time, I watched as the ice rink was littered with hats thrown for the crowd chanting his name and going nuts following his third goal.

Great. Not only did he ogle me with those sinfully gorgeous green eyes, but I had to clean up after his ass. As the door opened, the girls and I rushed to get the ice clean as fast as we could. In an arena with over fifteen thousand fans and sixty percent of them wearing hats, that wouldn't be as easy as it sounded. With each pile of hats I scooped up, I glared and cursed him as I watched him laughing and high-fiving his teammates.

Ugh, I hated the lot of them.

Especially the rookies. *Grrr.*

They were nothing but trouble. New players were all the same. They went around trying to prove something, fucking everything in their paths before leaving their bedmates in the dark. It was annoying, disgusting, and everything I hated about the sport of hockey. I used to be a fan—a huge fan, actually—when I lived in Minnesota. Not liking hockey wasn't very Minnesotan. Cheering for every hockey team from local high schools up to the pros was a done deal. That was our duty. It was what we did, and I did it well.

Of course, that all changed when I got involved with a player, and boom, things went to utter poo. Nasty poo. But I wasn't that girl anymore. I had moved to California with the drive to succeed as a sports therapist.

Why on earth would I end up back in hockey when I hate hockey players? Well, hockey is what I know. It was really only the antics *off the ice* that sparked my hate. As a physical therapist, I'd mostly be working with injured players, and they weren't the same at all. They were usually very driven, which I admired. There was a big difference between someone being a showboat—a guy who thought he was hot shit—and someone who was hurt but worked desperately to get back to the sport he loved. I enjoyed being around that type of hockey player, and I sure did love helping them.

Shaking my head, I looked around the arena full of people and bright lights, and exhaled hard. When I came to California for physical therapy school, I figured I'd work as a server in some restaurant and wait for my chance to intern, but that wasn't the way the Malibu Physical Therapy program worked. They placed students in internships right away. From day one I received hands-on training, and I loved it. I was especially thrilled when I learned I would be interning with the Malibu Suns, the Twin Cities Tornadoes' farm team.

During my orientation, I learned the Suns were hiring ice girls. I had done that in Minnesota, so I asked about it. To my surprise, I was hired on the spot. It was insane, but oh so awesome. I was studying a field I loved, had an awesome internship, and was working as both a skating instructor at the practice arena and an ice girl at the games. It was the perfect situation.

The downside, though, were the obnoxious rookies who assumed I was down to fuck. All the time.

Shoveling up another pile of hats, I cursed Gus again. My roommate Lizzy held the trash can. As we stuffed the hats in, she said, "Hopefully this is the only type of score he'll make."

"He's a douche."

Lizzy cracked up at that. "If you'd just give him a little bit, I bet it would be easier for you to chase him off." She paused and looked over at me. "Like you do everyone else."

I scoffed. "Fuck off. I do not chase everyone off."

"You do too," she insisted, shaking her head. "You've been here a year, and no dates, no boyfriends, no nothing. I don't even think you own a dildo."

"Ha. Little do you know, I have six."

"You freak!" she teased.

I beamed at her. Lizzy and I met our first day at MPT. We clicked instantly, and thankfully, she was looking for a roommate. I was living in on-campus housing, but my roommate was disgusting. She would throw dirty panties on the ground and leave them there for a week! Lizzy promised she cleaned, and that was enough to get me to quickly move in with her.

"All you do is work and go to school. We're in our twenties. We're supposed to be wild and free," she said.

I rolled my eyes. "I have things to do, a future to build. I'll be wild and free in my thirties."

"That's when you're supposed to have kids."

Her words evoked a sharp pang in my heart. By now I was practically a pro at ignoring that pain, so I waved her off, slamming a hat in the bin. "I'll push that back to my forties."

"So you can be sixty when they graduate? Ew, no."

"Hey, I'll be a *hot* sixty-year-old."

She laughed. "You're smoking now, girl!"

Lizzy was insane. All I could do was laugh as I scooped up hats with more force each time. I could hear Gus's voice as he boasted about how easy it was to score on the other team. He was freaking insufferable.

But as much as his ego infuriated me, and as obnoxious as he sounded joking with his teammates, I pictured his moss-green eyes and thick, gorgeous lashes. His rich brown hair was usually stuffed under a helmet, but when he wasn't on the ice, the long layers fell into his eyes. If his full lips and chiseled jaw weren't distracting enough, he had one of the finest bodies I had ever seen. I seriously hated how ripped he was. His sex appeal made me stupid, made me want to touch him. That was *not* going to happen. I knew damn well I needed to keep my distance from Gus Persson.

He was the kind of trouble I had been through, and I wouldn't go through again.

I couldn't.

"Don't worry, he won't be here long. Not with how much he is killing it. He'll be called up to the Tornadoes in no time," Lizzy said.

Something else moved in my chest—a different feeling than the sharp pang I felt earlier—but I ignored it and tried to suppress the emotion that threatened to shake my voice. "Good," I sputtered. "I hope he goes. We'll get a break from cleaning up hats."

Lizzy was right. Persson scored hat tricks left and right, which was unheard of for a defenseman. But then again, Persson wasn't your typical defenseman. He could just as easily play forward, but he really dominated on defense. He was a force to be reckoned with. I never understood how he'd gone third in the draft. My dad and I had discussed it for hours. It was insane for a player of his ability to go so late, but he did. The Suns were benefiting from his dominating skill, and eventually the Twin Cities Tornadoes would get the ultimate prize.

Not just Gus Persson...

The Cup.

Maybe?

Men who dominated games and cut down all competition around them used to turn me on. Not anymore. I already had a guy like that—someone out to show the world how great he was. Just as the thought crossed my mind, I spotted Gus trying to high-five players on the other team, completely proving my point.

He was just...*ugh*...obnoxious.

Not the kind of guy I wanted anywhere near me.

Nor had time for.

Even if he was sinfully hot.

And sexy.

And talented.

Glaring at him, I shook my head.

Jackass.

**This story continues in
Misadventures with a Rookie!**

ACKNOWLEDGMENTS

First and foremost we want to thank Meredith Wild for inviting us to join her on this journey and for being a valued friend to us ever since the beginning.

To Scott Saunders and the editing team, thank you for adding polish to our story so it could shine.

Thank you to Robyn for getting the word out about us and making sure we finally took that damn picture!

To the rest of the Waterhouse Press team, thank you for your patience, insight, and support.

Sarah Younger, thank you for keeping us organized and calm (a tall order for anyone). Your belief in us keeps us going.

An extra special thanks to Danielle and the InkSlinger community for helping us get out of our own way.

The Padded Room, thank you for supporting our craziness. From posting links, teasers, and helping get our name out there, you are a vital part of our dreams. We love you ladies!

To Erik, Mya, and Mason: Thank you for all the love you give me every day. You inspire me to push myself beyond what I ever thought was possible.

To Nick and Nolan: I couldn't love two guys more than

I love the two of you. Nick, you're the best Daddy, husband, and friend, and I love you more each day. Nolan, thank you for finally understanding that writing is one of Mommy's jobs and for letting me open a computer next to you without smashing all the keys.

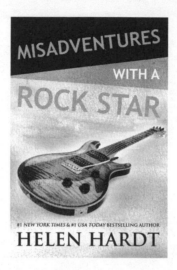

MORE MISADVENTURES